GAMES

— OF —

GREED

JO STEWART WRAY

STRATTON PRESS
We Celebrate Your Story

GAMES OF GREED
Copyright © 2022 **Jo Stewart Wray**

Stratton Press Publishing
831 N Tatnall Street Suite M #188,
Wilmington, DE 19801
www.stratton-press.com
1-888-323-7009

ISBN (Paperback): 978-1-64895-913-4
ISBN (Ebook): 978-1-64895-914-1

Printed in the United States of America

PROLOGUE

D uring a deadly plague that ravaged the earth, called the Silver Sickness, people had to stay home without going to schools, sporting events, and congregating in groups. They were desperate to be entertained. Borders were closed and anyone contracting the silver virus was contagious to everyone who breathed their air.

While pretending to educate the children, Honorable Governor Wade Johnson devised a plan to make himself rich while entertaining these people. Children (ages 12 to 18) were selected for an Underground Governor's School where they competed with each other for the entertainment of the above population.

Sadly, some of the losers disappeared from the competitions never to be seen again. Perhaps they contracted the Silver Sickness. Perhaps they didn't.

******

I see the painted red, white, and blue mail carrier jeep coming down Ratliff Street. Everyone in my neighborhood has matching mailboxes by direction of the Home Owners Association. Their homes are similar with only varying colors of brick or roof shingles. His brakes squeal as he stops at our mailbox. I am there as soon as he moves to the next mailbox. The letter is inside. The one I have been waiting on for days, the letter that could be my ticket out of the boring same one day after the next of being self-quarantined because of an invisible enemy, a Silver Sickness. The one that would change my life forever maybe for a good way, maybe for a bad. I grab it and yell loud enough for the neighbors across the street to hear, "Mama, it is here. It is addressed to you, Mrs. Thomas Freeman. It is from the governor, Honorable Governor Wade Johnson." My mama's hands shake as she opens the letter. There were many things about politicians that I didn't know or understand. Mama doesn't seem as happy about the letter as I am. The return address is Government Headquarters, 920 Capitol Street, Jackson, MS 55555. We went there once on a field trip when I was in elementary school. Of course, that was years ago before the Silver Sickness showed up in another country and made its way here. The envelope has an embossed seal in the left bottom corner, making it look official.

Dear Mrs. Freeman:

Due to the unprecedented and dangerous times we are living in, I've ordered all schools closed due to the Silver Sickness. Your daughter Sara has been selected to participate in a drawing to select who will attend the Honorable Governor's Capitol Underground School in what once was the casino underground Grand Americana Resort. Our curriculum includes sports which at regular schools can no longer have spectators, history of plagues, botany, coding, music, zoology, symbols, robotics, magic, mechanics, languages, medical/ potions, religions, photography, yoga, fishing and hunting, and self-defense. They may even see a few baby dragons. We will have six competing teams of diverse students from all areas of the state, and we would like Sara to be part of our student body. Our teams will be multi-levels and multi-ages.

We have transformed the Underground Grand America Casino into a beautiful, lush underground campus with a complete sports complex for competition swimming, a rock climbing wall, a skateboard park, and a self-defense pad. We even have a zoo filled with exotic animals. We have both girls and boys dormitories, teachers quarters, a shopping center (complete with a technology store, sports store, bookstore and a restaurant), classrooms, a museum, a bank, a zoo, a microbiology lab, and a quarantined area. The campus is on a beautiful underground island that few except the country's extremely rich have ever seen. Sara will be totally educated and ready for college when schools reopen after she returns home. It is a great honor to be selected to come to this school.

As of now, we will only have six or eight competing teams. We hope Sara is able to join our students in this fabulous adventure. Please watch channel 12 WABE TV on your television at 7:00 P.M. to see if Sara 's name is chosen.

Sincerely,

Wade Johnson

Wade Johnson
Governor of Mississippi

At 6:45 P.M., Mother and I sit on the couch, glued to the television. I rub my upper left shoulder since it throbs occasionally. It has become a habit like a nervous tic. I constantly rub my right hand over my throbbing left shoulder. I do not know why that shoulder throbs. I don't remember injuring it. We are glued to the television for different reasons. I'm so excited I can hardly contain it. My mother is horrified, but as usual she is letting me do whatever I want to within reason. We waited through the endless Medicare and dancing bears in toilet paper commercials for the drawing for who gets to attend the Governor's Underground School. I wonder why he didn't say I was accepted in the original letter.

My father Thomas Freeman died only two months before from horrific complications from the Silver Sickness. He was working for a pharmaceutical company that was developing a vaccine for the Silver Sickness that was killing many of the people it infected. The Silver Sickness gave flu-like symptoms, but anyone with an underlying pre condition often had attacks on their vital organs. He had been close to the final formula. Although I miss him terribly, I also miss my friends. I miss going to school and being around other people, especially others my age. Because of the deadly Silver Sickness, schools are closed until further notice, and I am home-schooled online. I'm only sixteen years old, and I am going into the eleventh grade. I crave social interaction.

At exactly seven o'clock P.M., loud music blares from the television. From the sound of the music, something important and exciting is about to happen. A group of uniformed people wearing white hazmat suits of protective material march six feet apart across the stage in front of the camera. They may be following rules by the PHO, Planet Health Organization. Honorable Governor Wade Johnson and his two secretaries stand six feet apart in front of the stage next to a table with an upturned top hat, a podium, and a microphone. The Honorable Governor Wade wears a double-breasted gray tweed suit although it is sweltering hot. He must have the air conditioner turned down to freezing. His skin looks scrubbed squeaky clean. Although masks are mandatory by order of the governor himself, Governor Johnson and his secretaries aren't wearing one. It is just one more of the ambiguities of these times. We are to wear masks but he doesn't. Do what I say; not what I do. I know he can't control the Silver Sickness. Nobody can.

"We are drawing today for the lucky students who will be going to our Governor's Capitol Underground Campus tomorrow morning," says one of the governor's secretaries, wearing a large flower on her lapel in a bright yellow color. She picks up the top hat and shakes it as if to mix the names. She acts official like she knows what she is doing. This secretary is dressed all in yellow linen-look fabric, the yellow color of a daffodil. Her skirt is yellow, her blazer is yellow, and her shoes are yellow with flowers on her toes. She says this in the slowest, southern drawl you can imagine, saying *waater* not water and *daaling* not darling. I think she must be from the Mississippi Delta.

"Tomorrow?" Mama asked, she pushes out her hands in front of her in a stopping motion. "But we aren't ready. I didn't think it would be so soon. I thought they would wait until August, the normal time for school to start after summer vacation."

"Don't worry mothers. No special preparations are necessary," Governor Johnson's secretary says in her slow drawl as if talking directly to my mother in the same room. Her tone is so sweet that if it were molasses you would have to heat the jar to get any out. "If your student's name is selected, we will pick him or her up in the morning from your front door. We already know everyone's addresses. He or she will also win a debit card to use on school supplies and clothing at our well-stocked store on the campus. So let us select our first name. Remember how lucky your student is to be selected. It is an honor. It is an advantage that can't be obtained anywhere else or in any other state or for any other place on our planet." She held the top hat toward the Honorable governor for him to select a name. I was thinking of the debit card and hoping the secretary dressed like a daffodil would be the one selecting our clothes. I was wondering if our uniforms would be bright yellow.

I look at my mother. She does not look relieved. She does not look happy. She looks as if she is praying that they won't select my name. She looks scared to death.

Our Honorable Governor Johnson sticks his hand into the open top hat full of names. He moves it around to stir them up. This is the first time he has spoken, but he does give a weak wave to the camera, making him look extremely ineffective or drugged. Maybe he's on our medical marajuana. "Our first student's name is Sara Freeman."

I hear nothing else that is said on the television show. "Oh, my, Mama, I'm going to the Governor's Capitol Underground Campus School, in the morning. I need to pack. I need to take a bath and shampoo my hair. I need a manicure and a pedicure." Then I look at my mother, "I need some money for school supplies, but I know we don't have any."

"I've got some cash tucked in under the mattress in our bedroom. I'll go get it. The letter says that they have a store on campus where you can get school supplies. His secretary just said that you will get a debit card to use. It will be better to get supplies there because we are still in that absurd stay-at-home order, so I can't go to the mall, but we don't have much money anyway. My federal stimulus check hasn't arrived, nor has the life insurance money I had on your father, Thomas. I will send you some more money through the bank on campus. Remember you have a Pay Pal account, so sending it will be digital.

"Oh, Mama. I'm scared. I don't want to leave you here alone," I say, reaching to hug my mother. "What if you get sick like daddy did? What if you get the Silver Sickness?" I don't know why they call it that. It should be called gray sickness. Remember how gray and lifeless it made daddy look as if he didn't have any blood running through his veins because someone had sucked it out, or he had been cut and it all ran out on the ground.

"But that underground school will be like school used to be here before the deadly Silver Sickness. It is just underground as in under the ground literally. So they can filter out the Silver Sickness from the air." Her voice cracks and a big tear shines in her eyes and rolls down her cheek. "You must take a cell phone with you. The one that used to be your father's will work. Oh, Sara, are you certain that you want to go? I'm going to miss you so terribly. I'm going to worry about you. So much could go wrong in this situation. I'm not even sure that I trust the Honorable Governor."

"Yes, Mama, I'm going to miss you, too. I will come back on our first break. We will probably have Fall Break in October like we usually do. Oh, Mama. Will you be okay without me?" I reach and hug my mother another time. I really love my mother. She smells like Ivory soap bodywash. "Did you hear any more names that were called? I was so excited that I quit listening after he called my name."

"Yes, Mike, the boy across in the next cul-de-sac. His name was called. You rode the school bus with him."

"Ugh. Mike Lawrence? I really don't like him. He is a bully on the school bus," I reply. I remember the last day on the bus that Mike had bullied this little girl until she cried into giving him her seat near the back. He never liked to sit near the front because the driver could watch what he was doing. The poor little girl moved toward the front and asked some other girls if she could sit with them. I felt so sorry for her. And we had assigned seats."

CHAPTER 2

At 8:00 the next morning, three people wearing white hazmat suits stand on our front porch. I move the curtain and peer at them through the window. They shift from one foot to another in an even, mechanical way. Our doorbell rings. I run to open the door. "We are here to pick up Sara Freeman, a student who was chosen to go to the Governor's Capitol Underground Campus School. Sara Freeman will not need any luggage. We will furnish everything Sara Freeman needs at the school," a female voice in the white suit said in a robotic voice. "She will get a governor's debit card for everything. The Honorable Governor's picture is on the front."

"I'm she. I'm Sara Freeman," I say. I am so nervous; I'm shaking. My left shoulder throbs. Nervously, I rub it with my right hand. I look at my mother. "She must take her cell phone, or she can't go," Mrs. Freeman says, gripping Sara with both arms around her. "I don't really want her to go anyway." The hazmat suits were rudely looking over our house as if trying to find something.

"Mrs. Freeman, it is by order of Honorable Governor Wade Johnson that Sara Freeman go with us. Everyone in the entire state must follow his orders. He is the duly elected governor. She can bring her phone, but there is not any cell service underground and charging it may be a problem some of the time because all the electricity is used to run the lights for the campus and filter the air. We are underground in total darkness unless the florescent lighting system is on. Maybe she will need a charging brick."

"Why are you doing this?" Mrs. Freeman asks. "Governor Wade Johnson is becoming a dictator." Tears roll down her face. I hug my mother tightly. She is acting like I will never return. She always worries prematurely. I guess that is what mothers do, but I wish she would stop embarrassing me and stop saying bad things about Governor Wade.

"The Honorable Governor has provided these students with a grand opportunity to be schooled without fear of catching the Silver Sickness. She will be on a team with other students and will be educated. Then she will be allowed to compete against other teams that the governor has selected. Think of it as boarding school, Mrs. Freeman. Free boarding school that is like school used to be before the Silver Sickness, but this one is better than any other high school." Her voice is kind but robotic as if she has rehearsed what to say many times.

Reluctantly, Mother releases me. She lets me go with these white hazmat suited, robotic people. "What if Sara doesn't want to compete? What if your power goes out? What if she gets sick? How can I know that she is safe? Why aren't they teaching the normal courses for high school like algebra, biology, English, and history? Are there really dragons there? Isn't that dangerous? Why are you teaching magic?"

"We are here to pick up Sara Freeman, who was selected to go to the Governor's Capitol Underground Campus School. Sara Freeman will not need any luggage. We will furnish everything she needs at the school," the same female voice in the white suit says as if the message was prerecorded. "Put on this mask, Sara Freeman." The white suit hands me the mask inside a sealed paper wrapping.

"No, I've changed my mind," my mother screams. "I'm calling the police. She can't go. This is America. She can not go. I don't care what the governor says."

"Go ahead. We are the police," one of the male hazmat suits said, fitting a mask over my nose and mouth. I fainted as if it had chloroform. "You have had twelve hours to tell Sara goodbye. This is an official mandate by the Governor. You have no choice."

"No, I know some of the police. Why, one policeman lives across the street," my mother says and picks up a heavy glass vase from the table in the hallway and strikes the talking male hazmat white suit in the face, but the female white suit drags my limp body outside and down the sidewalk to the armored truck, parked out front next to the our mailbox. I barely know what is happening. She loads me inside and slams the door shut. I hear my mother scream. "Let go of me. I'm calling the police."

They leave my mother melting into a puddle of tears and emotion on our front porch. I wonder if the neighbors are watching. I look at their windows and see a slight movement of the curtains. Seeing her in that shape makes emotion catch in the back of my throat. I hope my mother survives without me and my father to take care of her. I hope they don't come back and arrest her for hitting that white hazmat person. I hope I have been so selfish. I hide my face in my hands so that the robots won't see my tears. I don't want the other students in the bus to see the evidence of my tears either.

CHAPTER 3

The white van that looked like an armored vehicle that banks transported money in drove down the street and into the next cul-de-sac to pick up Mike Lawrence. They escort him to the van and put him in the seat in the vehicle next to me. He wears all black and a mask too, but I knew where he lived, so recognizing him was easy. His hair is jet black, and he has a mean look in his black eyes. He smells of Old Spice aftershave, but he isn't old enough to shave much. I look at the stubble on his chin. My grandmother would have called him a little upstart shaver with peach fuzz. He hasn't started to shave yet. Mike has been in some of my classes, so I figured he is about my age. His mother isn't out on the porch demanding for him to stay home.

"Well, lookie here," he says. "If it isn't the ugliest girl in my school. You need to wear a mask all the time. It improves your looks." I imagine the smirk behind his mask.

"Shut up," I say. "You are such a bully. Didn't your mother teach you not to be a bully? Did you bring your cell phone?" Suddenly, I'm obsessed with cell phones. There is a large knot in the pit of my stomach as if a large group of butterflies are flying in circles.

Before he can answer, all three white suits climb back into the vehicle and we ride away. He pats his pocket and nods. I look out the windows of the vehicle, but hadn't been able to see inside through the tint. To me it is tinted darker than the legal limit. I want to see if Mike has his cell phone in his pocket because he lies a lot. I wonder where we are headed. I don't know where the entrance to that Underground Casino is. At 16, I'm too young to go into a casino except to eat, and my parents didn't gamble. I look out the window, but I can't tell where they are going until they drive south onto Interstate 55 and then exit.

They turn off onto High Street, drive west to downtown Jackson, and then drive through the gates and park next to the Governor's Mansion. All the white hazmat suits exit the car in one sweep and go inside a side door of the mansion, leaving me and Mike locked inside the white van.

"Do you have a cell phone? Isn't it illegal to leave us locked in a hot car? We could die." I say.

"Yes, I do have a phone, you dumb girl," Mike replies. "But I'm not letting you use up all my minutes. Where is yours?"

"Oh, I have my father's. Mine is unlimited time and data. "I gaze outside at the manicured grounds of the Governor's Mansion. Someone must work on these grounds constantly. There isn't even a leaf or blade of grass out of its designated place. There aren't any people around, but the azaleas are blooming and so is the magnolia tree. I smell its sweet perfume. Of course, the Governor's Mansion would have magnolia trees. Magnolias are the state flower of Mississippi.

At that moment, the white hazmat suits come back to the car and take me and Mike inside the Governor's Mansion and immediately to an elevator that has no windows. We ride down several levels. Somehow that sweet smell from the magnolia blooms or something is making me sick. The door of the elevator opens to a rail station. We are herded to the front of a silver, bullet-shaped railcar without any windows. The robotic female in the white hazmat suit leads us to the entrance to a railcar, shows us where to sit and buckles us tightly in our seats. The seatbelt is more like a harness than a regular seat belt. It comes across my chest and across my waist. Another one crisscrosses the first one. This reminds me of rides at the state fair or Disney World. She says nothing. Immediately upon getting us harnessed into our seats, the white hazmat suit leaves.

"Do you really want to do this?" I ask Mike. I try to keep my voice even and steady. I don't want him to know how afraid I am. "I mean, do you really want to go to The Governor's Underground School?"

"Sure I do. My father works for Governor Wade. It is going to be fun. I'm excited. I'm going to get special treatment at this school. I will get top grades. Then I will get a college scholarship. You just wait. I will have help from the teachers because of my dad. Besides online school is dumb. Except for nerds like you who stay online all the time on the dumb social media sites. Shut up. Stop talking to me, you dumb girl."

"Something other than educating us is going on here. Don't you think?" I look directly at him and notice that he had a large red whelp on one cheek. Maybe that is why his mother didn't come out on the porch. "What happened to your face?"

"I told you that my father works for Governor Johnson." He is avoiding my question about his face. "My dad is even going to be working at the Capitol Underground Campus. He is going to teach there. He is excellent at self-defense. I'm taking that class. I can't wait." Mike gloats. "I'm already pretty good. I took ju jitsu."

"No, you didn't. You couldn't have. If you took ju jitsu, you would know that bullying is bad," I reply. Anger makes my voice stronger even through the mask.

"Shut up, dumb girl."

"I am definitely not dumb," I say. "You'll find out."

"Oh, yeah, a nerd."

At that time the silver, bullet-shaped railcar begins to fill with more students. They take their seats in alternating rows as suggested by the CDC guidelines or PHO to socially distance. Although there are some vacant seats left, some of the students spill over into the next few railcars, but all are ushered through this car first. I don't see how that is safe since according to the guidelines the Silver Sickness is airborne.

I look at each one as they enter, but don't recognize anyone else. Perhaps it is because they wear masks. A pale blonde girl is harnessed in her seat across from me, so I introduce myself.

"Hi, I'm Sara. Do you have a cell phone?" I ask her. She looks scared to death. Her face is flushed, and she is biting her fingernails.

"Yes, I have one in my sports bra in a specially designed pocket? Why? Don't you?" the pale girl softly answers. Her voice is low and squeaky. She looks to be about twelve years old and absolutely terrified. "I'm scared. I have never even spent the night away from my parents except with my grandmother." A big tear rolls down her face. "I'm Emelia Smith. I'm in the sixth grade."

"I'm scared too," I admit. "I've been sitting on my hands to keep from biting my nails. Maybe we are in the same dormitory and can be friends." This little girl looks too small to even wear a sports bra or even have a cell phone, but if I were a mother, I would make certain my daughter had a cell phone. I haven't had one long. My cell used to belong to my father. She looks to be at least four years younger than I am.

"I would like that. My name is Sara Grace Freeman. I'm in high school. Emelia. That's a beautiful name. I'm just called Sara. Well, I was going to Malmason next year before they put it all online. I don't know much about this new school we are going to. Do you?"

"No, I don't. And all this is very frightening and exciting too. It is good to have a new friend, Sara. I'm glad to meet you," Emelia says, her green eyes glisten because they are filled with tears.

The silver bullet railcar starts suddenly and whizzes down the rails through the tunnel at lightening speed, throwing Emelia and me back into our seats. "I bet we are going 200 miles an hour. I don't like this," Emelia says.

"Me neither," I answer. Suddenly, everything goes black." It is like riding a ride at the fair or Disney World and going through a tunnel."

The silver bullet railcar's lights come on and flood the darkness. A voice comes over a speaker saying, "We have reached our destination, The Capitol Underground School Campus. You will be taken to the Quarantine Area/Prisons where you will be housed in quarantine for two weeks. It is located at the backside of the island where the railcar station ends. You will get a tour of the campus only if you are allowed to stay here. You will stay here only if you don't come down sick within those two weeks of quarantine. You will be tested daily for Silver Sicknesses. You must wear a mask at all times until it is proven that you are not infected. After two weeks of quarantine, you will be transported to your sleeping quarters at the school campus."

"I wonder what happens if we get sick. Did he say Quarantine/Prisons? What school needs a prison? For that matter, what casino? We only had detention at our school and in-school-suspension," Emelia says.

"Yes, I heard that too," I answer. A larger knot tightens in my stomach.

"I wonder when our Fall Break is?" I am already eager to get out of here.

"Unfasten your seatbelts," a voice on the speaker says. "Make sure you are correctly wearing the mask you were given, meaning covering your mouth and your nose, and line up at least six feet apart. We are carrying you to the Quarantine Area. First, we will check your temperature before you get to exit this silver bullet railcar." I wonder why they didn't check our temperatures before we entered. Then those with a temp could have been taken back home.

We get in line like we are instructed and leave on our masks. Suddenly, extremely bright lights flood the island. I squint my eyes and shade them. The lights resemble sunshine in brightness but are florescent. A sound of something overhead sliding closed whishes. I want to ask Emelia if she heard it, but the mask and distance we are apart prevent communication.

I guess it is a ceiling dome overhead, I decide. Perhaps it keeps the dragons out or maybe inside. I gaze upward, but the bright lights prevent my vision. Maybe it helps with the heating and cooling of the island. It might keep other things in and out. I wonder if rocks fall. The island appears to be very large. It is much larger than I anticipated, but that is a good thing.

About that time one of the hazmat suits points a digital thermometer in my direction. Then I am allowed to exit the steps of the bullet railcar. I reach the bottom step then I am stopped near a tent by more people in white hazmat suits. A number is pinned to my chest. "You are number 600. You must wear your number at all times." Then the white hazmat suit yells to the suits inside the tent. "Are you ready to test the next one? Number 600."

I am told to sit down and lean my face upward. A eight inch Q-Tip like instrument is stuck far up my nose and scrapes the inside of my sinus cavity. It hurts. I feel like they scraped my brain. "Number 600 Freeman," the guy says. The test is slipped inside a plastic tube and sealed.

I am instructed to stand six feet away from the other students as they test more students. Finally, we are marched down a new concrete sidewalk for about two blocks. Emelia walks lightly... almost sound-lessly behind me. When we reach the quarantined area building, it is surrounded by a chain link fence with barbed wire strung across the top. It does look like a prison. We are handed a bag of paper cloth-ing and some paper slippers and instructed to change into them. They tell us that our clothing is to be thrown away.

"I want to keep my Nike shoes. They are new," Emelia pleads. "They were a gift from my grand-mother for my birthday."

"Well, you can not," replied the white hazmat suit. "They may be contaminated. They will be burned with the rest of these contaminated clothes and shoes. Take them off and give them to me now."

"But what shoes will I wear? " Emelia asks.

"If you get out of quarantine without coming down with an infection, you may purchase more Nike shoes just like these. If not, you will not need shoes where you will be taken." The hazmat suit's voice sounds dead and robotic, except there is a slight smirk in her tone.

"I don't want different Nikes. I want the ones my grandmother gave me. "

"Where do we go if we don't get out of quarantine?" I ask. "Do we go back home?"

"No. You must win the competition to get the Silver Sickness vaccine. These competitions are survival of the fittest. If you have the Silver Sickness, you may not go back above the earth with the rest of the population."

The knot in my stomach grows larger. I start a diary on my phone. Well, I will as long as the battery lasts. Before I left home, my mother made me charge it to 100% and the charging brick too.

Day 1 Quarantine

I start a log/diary on my phone.

I turn the power off immediately after entering into my online journal. There is no charging outlet in the quarantined tent. A cell phone may be my best friend. I hope Emelia keeps hers off, too, to conserve the battery.

After changing into the paper shoes and clothes, all of us students except one are instructed to go into the rooms with our numbers/name on the door. My friend Emelia is number 601. Our rooms are sealed glass tents with cots and paper sheets and no pillows. I miss my pillow from home. I miss my mother. I miss cheeseburgers. Food here is prepackaged and drops down a chute with plastic utensils. Each room has its own bathroom.

We are instructed to shower at 7:30 P.M. Lights are turned out at 8:00 P.M.

Where did that one student with a temperature go? He was male, but he wasn't Mike.

Day 2 Quarantine

I am awakened at 6:00 A.M. by bright lights and the blaring intercom with, "Wishing you the best and a very bright future. You should be honored to be here." The white suits show up and my temperature is taken with that digital thermometer. We are tested for Silver Sicknesses. The test still hurts. A prepackaged egg sandwich and a sealed cup of milk drop down the tube. The sandwich is warm, but the milk is cold. Weird. I wonder how that works.

Lunch is a vegetable burger and cold milk.

Dinner is the same. The florescent lights definitely are bright.

Otherwise, I see no one. I sit or lie on the cot with the paper sheet and no pillow. I wait. I wonder where the boy is that had a temperature. I wonder if he tested positive for a Silver Sickness. I wonder about my new friend Emelia. I wonder how my mom is. I miss her. I sneak out my cell phone to call her, but I don't have any service. I have zero bars. I wonder if she has tried to call me or left a message or text. I don't have an outlet to charge my phone.

A book is dropped down the chute. It lands on the counter pad with a thud. The sound would have scared me if I hadn't heard it coming. It is titled The *History of Plagues*. My name is not yet inside the cover. The book smells of Clorox bleach or Lysol spray. I don't know which. I again wonder about the boy who tested positive for the Silver Sickness, the one with a temperature.

Day 3 Quarantine

I am awakened at 6:00 A.M. by bright lights and the blaring intercom with, "Wishing you the best and a very bright future." They had dropped the, "You should be honored to be here." I fell asleep while reading The *History of Plagues*. It is boring, but there is nothing else to do. I definitely do not feel honored to be here.

The white suite shows up to take my temp and test for Silver Sicknesses.

Breakfast is the same.

Lunch is the same.

Dinner is the same.

I am bored. My phone still has no bars, but I turn the power on it just in case. I turn it on just long enough to journal.

Day 4 Quarantine

I am awakened at 6:00 A.M. by bright lights and the blaring intercom with, "Wishing you the best and a very bright future." I fell asleep while reading The History of Plagues. It is the same as yesterday. It is boring, but there is nothing else to do.

The white suit shows up to take my temp and test for Silver Sicknesses. I am tired of these tests, but I'm scared to test positive like that boy did. I don't want to disappear, and I don't want the Silver Sickness.

Breakfast is the same.

Lunch is the same.

Dinner is the same.

Day 5 Quarantine

I am still here. I am bored. What day is this? They are all the same.

Day 6 Quarantine

Everything is the same except now the white suits actually say, "Wishing you the best and a very bright future."

I don't reply. How do you talk to robots? I still don't feel honored to be here.

Day 7 Quarantine

I woke before the bright lights came on. I wish this would end. I want my mother.

I don't want to disappear like that boy who had a temperature. His disappearance worries me.

I think of my mother. I miss her.

Suddenly, the bright lights come on and "Wishing you the best and a very bright future."

The rest of the day is the same.

Day 8 Quarantine

It is the same, but I finished the book. It was very boring. I am tired of the same food. I miss my mother.

Day 9 Quarantine

Last night I dreamed about my father. I dreamed about this sickness known as the Silver Sickness. He was rushed to the hospital, and we couldn't go see him. He was on a ventilator. He died from a blood clot after being in the hospital for weeks. I miss him too.

The rest of the day is the same. The day is long.

Day 10 Quarantine

Today is the same as yesterday. I hate "Wishing you the best and a very bright future." The only thing bright here is the lights.

Day 11 Quarantine

Same. One of the white suits has dirt on his suit. I wonder why.

Day 12 Quarantine

Same.

Day 13 Quarantine

I will never eat another vegetable burger. I eat the bread and flush the vegetable patty down the commode.

Same except my left shoulder throbs.

Day 14 Quarantine

At 6:00 A.M. the bright lights come on. The intercom blares, "Wishing you the best and a very bright future."

The white suits show up. This time there are three of them. All three have dirt on their suits.

"You have passed our tests. You have not tested positive for Silver Sicknesses and haven't had a temp. Tomorrow one of us will take you to order your school supplies, laptop computer or Ipad, shoes, textbooks, uniforms, and clothes, and to get you signed up for classes. Then you will be taken to your sleeping quarters on the other end of the island.

At 3:00, you will board a government shuttle bus for a tour of your new, underground island home, the Governor's Underground School. Dinner will be at exactly 6:00 P.M. Remember to wear your number at all times. Here is your identification badge. Let me write your name in your history book, " he says.

I am so scared that I can hardly contain myself. I am truly ready for quarantine to be over, but I need to talk to my mother to tell her that I'm okay. I wanted to inquire about the boy who had a temperature. Where did he go?

Day 15 Out of Quarantine

The white suit that was assigned to me comes to get me this morning. All I'm allowed to do is to follow him.

CHAPTER 4

My personal white hazmat suit helps me into a golf car beside him or maybe it is a her. I can't really tell. He hands me a debit card. The governor's picture is on the front in living color. In the picture, he is still wearing the double-breasted gray tweed suit. He wears small horn-rimmed glasses, and his skin isn't very weathered, but it is ruddy and has a shine. Actually, his face is so red that my grand-mother would have asked him if his blood pressure was elevated. She hated a ruddy complexion. Instead, he has a baby face, making him look very young. " Use this to buy whatever you need." I've never had my own debit card before. I am embarrassed to have on paper clothes, but we ride on a sidewalk across a heavily forested area and I don't see anyone else along the way. I don't feel so naked. Dim lights light the sidewalk. I thought about how much electricity it takes to light, heat, and cool this place. The first store we go into is a clothing store. Other students wearing paper clothes are there too. I feel a little better, except the bully Mike Lawrence is there. He glares at me and snickers, sounding much like a horse. He wears what I assume is to be our school uniform. He wears a white polo shirt and khaki pants. I'm glad it isn't daffodil yellow like the governor's secretary's clothes.

"First, we will get you some clothing and shoes," my white hazmat suit mentor says. I wonder why he still wears the white hazmat suit, but I don't ask.

After picking out some school uniforms - khaki pants, white polo shirts- underwear, and canvas shoes. I slip into the dressing room lined with mirrors and put on underwear and a set of the uniform clothing, white polo shirt and khaki pants. I realize that boys and girls dress the same. My outfit matches Mike's. Whenever I come out of the dressing room, the white hazmat suit has picked out a lab coat for me. Raising my left shoulder causes it to throb. There was no need for an outer coat because this entire campus is a large controlled temperature environment. I guess it never rains either. Although I don't like the looks of the uniform, I am so happy to get out of the paper clothes. The uniforms are a welcome change. We weren't required to wear uniforms at my other school, but I can see that this Governor's Capitol Underground School is going to be very different.

Next, the white hazmat suit says, " We must get your technology and sports equipment now. We must get your textbooks and school supplies, too. It is very important that your team scores high in as many categories as possible. The team who wins the overall score of the competition gets to take the vaccines back to their county, friends, and family first before the general population, including health care workers and the elderly. There is a possibility that there isn't enough vaccine to go around. Your father worked for the Pitman company who was developing a vaccine. Did he ever talk about his work? We need a vaccine for the elderly. Their lives may be saved if the second or third round of these Silver Sicknesses hits. It might be a matter of life or death to someone you know like your grandparents."

"Hi, Sara," a soft voice said. "Sara? Sara?"

I was thinking about what the suit had said about the vaccine and my grandmother. So this is a competition for a vaccine for my county, family, and friends. Somehow, that seems bogus. My father had been working on a vaccine, but had contracted the Silver Sickness himself and died. I wonder if there won't be enough vaccine for everyone. This is a governmental power game. I sound like my Aunt Rebecca. She is always telling people to "Wake Up, America!" She wants them to side with the President and not to believe the news media or "Fake News" as she calls it. I'm beginning to think that she is right.

"Sara?" It is Emelia.

"Oh, how are you?"

"Glad to be out of that boring quarantine cubby. Aren't you?"

The white hazmat suit walks away from us. Clearly, he isn't into being social. Just social distancing. But none of us should have a Silver Sickness. We have been in quarantine for two weeks.

The white hazmat suit walks into the sports equipment store. I follow. "Now, let us get your equipment. Which sport are you doing first? Skateboarding, mountain climbing, swimming, or self-defense?" the white suit asks. " I suggest self-defense."

"I was thinking about skateboarding." I answer, heading toward some skate boards hanging on the wall. I remember Mike saying he wanted to take self-defense, and I want to stay as far away from him as possible for as long as possible. I wonder how bullies will be handled at this school. If his father is one of the teachers, I figure he would be a bully too. My grandmother used to say, "The apple doesn't fall far from the tree."

The white hazmat suit helps me select a skateboard and another pair of rubber-soled shoes with plastic shoe lace protectors. My Ultimate Dream skateboard is bright pink and has a larger deck than I have ridden before. I get tie-dyed tee shirts, pants, and a hooded sweatshirt to match, making me a big blob of hot pink. There is no way I will blend in with a crowd. I notice that Emelia also got outfitted for skateboarding. Hers is lime green with bright yellow stripes. I feel so sorry for her. She misses her parents terribly. I miss my mother too, but I'm old enough to be over the homesickness. I guess I will always miss my father.

Then the white suit and I buy all the textbooks on the list except Photography, History of Magic, and History of Religion. They are set to come in later in the semester. Some of the classes such as: robotics, symbols, zoology, yoga, photography, mechanics, fishing, hunting, magic, and decoding seem interesting. I notice that he gets me books for every class listed, even those that I'm not taking. That puzzles me, but I don't ask any questions. My interest definitely will depend on the teacher's personality. I figure we will meet our teachers at dinner in the cafeteria. I am not as interested in music, botany, and the history of plagues now. I read the book History of Plagues. It is so boring.

We go outside and load all my merchandise into the back seat of our golf cart where the golf bags usually go. Then we go to the technology store to get a lap top. I get a Dell with an up-to-date processor instead of an Ipad. "I can't wait to get this set up in my room, so I can message my mother." I say aloud.

"The rules prevent contacting parents directly," the white hazmat suit says. "If you try it to email them or message them on social media, your laptop will be taken, leaving you to do your school work without it. Reports are periodically sent to your parents by the Governor's office, but there is a special channel where your parents can watch the competitions to keep up with you, but no correspondence between you is allowed. People will be betting on the outcome of the all the competitions, and whichever team loses will have a team member removed. Finally, there will be one winner.

I want to ask about the little boy who disappeared, but I'm afraid. I may do some searching on my own.

The time is around 2 o'clock, so the white hazmat suit drives me across the campus to my dormitory. We ride through the zoo, past the museum, and across the food court. The animals in the zoo aren't any I've ever seen before. That is strange. Smelling the food at the food court reminds me that I missed lunch, but the white hazmat suit doesn't seem to be hungry. I guess robots don't eat. They just get their batteries recharged. Finally, after passing the self-defense pad, we reach the student's sleeping quarters. I am in section 12 and number 600 is on my door. I noticed that Emelia is also in my section. I also notice that there are electrical outlets near the bed. I am glad.

After three loads from the golf cart, clothes, shoes, books, and all the rest is inside the building. We walk up a long, carpeted staircase that opens at the top into a large, floral carpeted seating area with a brick fireplace and black flocked wallpaper of the walls on one end that isn't windows. Commons' Area. The huge glass windows can be closed or opened and heavy velvet drapes with fringe that can be drawn to keep out the bright lights that simulate sunlight. The seating area reminds me of a study hall/library/book-store with overstuffed, blue leather chairs grouped together near small mahogany end tables and mahogany study tables and with four or six chairs for each where groups can sit to converse or study. Signs with the rules for this area are posted. The three exterior walls are covered with shelves filled with books. Down a hallway is a room that leads to our sleeping quarters, and we all share a large bathroom with showers at the end of the hall. The predominant color scheme is green in various shades. To enter the sleeping area, there is a facial recognition machine to unlock the door. The white hazmat suit helps me set this to recognize my face.

"Meet the small yellow bus out front at 3:00 P.M." the white hazmat suit says. "You will get a tour of the campus. Then a grand buffet dinner in the grand room down stairs on the first floor, you will meet the teachers and the headmaster. You will hear the competition rules and rewards."

"Will the Honorable Governor Wade Johnson be there?" I ask.

"Oh, no. He just watches everything on his video intercom whenever he chooses. He is very tech savvy. He is very secretive. He is far too busy to attend anything here. He will send live television announcements from time to time," the male white hazmat suit says. "So do not ever do anything that he should not see. There are cameras everywhere. Remember this was a casino. Oh, yes, I forgot. You aren't old enough to have ever gone in a casino, but you watch television, so I'm sure you understand."

CHAPTER 5

Suddenly, the white hazmat suit robot leaves, and Emelia and a group of students pour into the Common's Area. "Oh, Sara," Emelia said. "Our sleeping quarters are next to each other. I'm so glad. I'm adopting you as my big sister. I don't have any brothers and sisters. I like our sleeping quarters with the white sheets and fluffy white comforters. We actually have a pillow and pillowcase. And we have pillows, big fluffy pillows."

"Awe, Emelia. Thank you," I answer. My arms are full of textbooks. "Do you like it better here now? Let's go outside. I just saw the bus coming to take us on the tour of the campus. "If we don't have to sit in any particular spot on the bus, will you sit next to me?" We get on the bus and move into the first two seats behind the driver. Maybe Mike will sit near the back.

The tour starts as soon as the students fill the bus. I hear Mike bragging loudly in the back. First, the bus heads toward the Sports Complex. Then we ride past a skateboard park with concrete ramps curving toward the sky, a mountain climbing wall or boulder, an Olympic-sized swimming pool, and the self-defense pad.

The Sports Complex is surrounded by an electric fence. I hear or maybe actually feel the buzz in the wires. Actually, it looks as if the entire island is also surrounded with a fence.

"I like it better, maybe a little. Do you?" Then we ride past the museum, the zoo, a small, red brick building housing an ATM, the mall, and the Outer Limits that looks like a graveyard of sorts, the forested area, the classrooms, and back to the sleeping quarters. Why would an underground campus need a graveyard? We don't stop at our sleeping quarters, but turn and ride past an extravagant building that houses The Headquarters, a Train Station, Microbiology Labs, Magic Labs, Robotics section, an electric power station, and the Quarantined/Prison area. They turn the corner and drive back through the thickly forested area, past the classrooms, and back to where we began.

"It is okay."

"This campus is laid out in about twelve main squares. Each contains an important function of our campus," the robotic tour guide says in a robotic, monotone. "When you exit the bus, please make your way to the grand cafeteria that is on the bottom floor below the sleeping quarters."

When we get back to our sleeping area, I enter an audio map of the island into my phone. Then we hurry to the cafeteria. I notice that my father has lots of pictures in the phone, but I don't have time to look at them now.

As we enter the grand cafeteria and find a seat, I say, "If I could talk to my mom, I might." All of a sudden a large commotion breaks out in the front of the room. A giant screen is being set up or rather pulled down from the ceiling. There are large, colorful silk banners hanging from the ceiling. I notice the maroon and blue ones.

"Ladies and gentlemen, welcome. We are going to watch a film about the Silver Sickness. Like your parents watch the news each evening, we are watching films about the Silver Sickness every day. We will see the numbers of those infected above ground daily. We will learn any updates or changes in the sickness.

"I hate the news," Emelia whispers. She leans over close enough to me so that no one else hears her.

"Me too," I answer. "Have you wondered why the robots wear hazmat suits? It seems to be a stupid idea to me. It the Silver Sickness is spread by air, how can a robot get sick?

"Silver Sicknesses: the State of the above Population."

"My father died of the Silver Sickness," I whisper to Emelia. Since we made it through quarantine, we can sit close together.

"Oh, Sara, I'm so, so sorry. I didn't know," Emelia answers.

Finally a new slide flashes across the screen and I covertly photograph each slide. Governor Wade gives us our rules to live by while at The Governor's

Underground School. They are going to call the school G.U. S. for short.

"These are the rules here:

1. No one is to contact their parents.

After that rule flashes up on the screen, a young, blonde boy with curls in his hair who sits near the back begins to have a panic attack. He falls out of his chair and begins squirming on the floor, gasping. Two of the robotic white hazmat suits come to get him and lead him away.

"Why are they still wearing hazmat suits?" Sara whispers. "I don't understand."

After that has quieted down, the next rule flashes up on the screen.

2. We are sending reports of your behavior and scores from your competitions to your parents every week.

3. Parents can tune in to Channel 12 WABE this week on their television to watch you practice the sports you are taking and to watch the competitions. They will be notified whenever the games and competitions are being televised. A schedule may be printed so they can arrange their busy schedules.

4. Try your best. People are betting their money on your success. This is part of the

State Lottery, but bets come from all over the globe.

5.   One person on the over-all winning team will get the vaccines for their county, family, and friends first before the general population and in some cases instead of the general population. Then your lives will be easier and like they used to be. Others may die from a second round of infection and/or mutations of the Silver Sickness. All Silver Sicknesses mutate.

All losing teams will have one person removed from their team by the Headmaster at the selection of Governor Wade.

6.   Any demerits will deduct from your team's scores. Teachers may give demerits as they see fit.

7.   Unless there are unusual circumstances, there will be no breaks to go home until a vaccine is developed and an overall team winner is determined.

8.   Parents or supporters or sponsors can send you money via Pay Pal, Cash App, Venmo, etc.

The film ends with a screen of the Honorable Governor Wade and a group of people wearing white hazmat suits surrounding him saying , "Wishing you the best and a bright future. You are honored to be here." He isn't wearing a mask. As the screen rises, I hide my phone.

A buzz starts in the cafeteria. "I'm gonna beat all these dumb girls," Mike says to the two creepy looking boys Ziegfred and Floyd who have become his shadow at the school. Ziegfred has stringy, long hair, parted in the center, and Floyd wears a crew-cut and has acne. "My father is going to teach self-defense. I know I'm going to win that competition."

"I'm taking skateboarding," Emelia whispers. "Me too." And I realize that she didn't want to be around Mike and those guys either.

At the front of the teacher's table and directly behind where the screen was dropped, a distinguished looking man with a chest length beard clinks his knife against his water glass, making a high pitched sound of metal on glass. "May I have your attention. I need to introduce your teachers. First, I will start with myself, I'm Headmaster Peeples, and I now will introduce the coaches because some think competition in sports will make this program because of the bets the above population can place on how the competitions go. Headmaster Peeples strokes his facial hair. For skateboarding, your coach is Nadia Calmanich, for mountain climbing is also Nadia Calmanich, for swimming is Olympic winner Chana Breeves, and for Self-Defense is Michael Lawerence, Sr. His son Mike is a student here. For Yoga, your instructor is Ashley House. For History of Magic we have Professor Tim Clean, for Mechanics we have

Professor Trade, for Languages Professor Melania, for Potions Mrs. Tim Clean, for Religion Dr. Jay Blue, for Photography Professor Lamb, for Hunting and Fishing the MS Dept. of Wild Life will instruct.

Our History of Plagues teacher is Elmira James who also wrote the book *History of Plagues* that you had to read during quarantine."

Each professor stands or waves whenever his or her name is mentioned. The professor's introductions take at least half an hour, and I am not going to remember who is who. I hope they wear name tags.

"Ugh,ugh," a large groan goes through the crowd. Headmaster Peeples clinks his glass to regain attention again.

"Our coding teacher is Sergeant John Smith." Smith stands and moves to the row of teachers in front of the speaker, and Zoology will be taught by a pair from Ole Miss, the Kendalls, and finally, robotics will be taught by an engineer named Professor Love. Finally, I am your headmaster, Professor Peeples. As you leave the cafeteria after dinner, pick up your schedules from the tables near the exit. Mrs. Jeannie, wearing hot pink clothes and having flaming red hair, will find your schedule. Mrs. Jeannie is over beside the door. Just give her your name. All classes begin at 8:00 A.M. in the center square of the campus unless we are having a competiton. Most of those are held in the grand cafeteria while all students are together. Some will be televised so that the folks above ground can watch and bet on them. You rode past it on your tour this evening. Some of the competitions will be held in other areas."

Robots enter the room with large trays piled high with food. It isn't prepackaged like that we had during quarantine. It looks like home-cooked, Sunday or Christmas or Thanksgiving dinner. There are large platters of fried chicken that smell heavenly, buttery, creamed potatoes with gravy, southern-style biscuits, peas, sweet tea, and large apple cobblers. Large bowls of bread and butter pickles like my mother used to make were set in the center of the tables. After the prepackaged and tasteless food we had been eating in quarantine, this looks delicious. The robots never speak one word, but I knew that their voices would be the same as those white hazmat suits voices had been. They are one and the same.

The plates are edged in gold and are white in the center. Emelia and I eat as much as we can before it is time to leave, and on the way out we pick up our schedules. Both of us have been starving since we have been quarantined for two weeks eating soybean burgers. Then we walk back up the brightly, floral carpeted stairs to the Common's Area.

"Let's compare our schedules," Emeilia says. "Let's see what we are taking together."

"I have skateboarding and I know you do too because I saw you buying a skateboard. Then I have botany, microbiology, robotics, magic, photography, yoga, and symbols," I say. "Let's go to our rooms before the others get up there." We slip up the heavily carpeted stairs, and I use my facial recognition for the door to open. I open the door to my room, and Emelia and I go inside and sit down on my fluffy white bed.

"Let me look at your schedule," I say, taking it from Emelia. "Let's see. We have skateboarding at the same time. Then you have botany whenever I have coding. We have micro together, then you have music while I have robotics, and then we both have symbols. You have all your textbooks and school supplies; don't you?"

"Yes," Emelia answers. " So we have skateboarding, microbiology, magic, photography, yoga, and symbols together. I guess we don't start photography or history of magic until second term. At least, I will know someone in some of my classes. I'm still so scared. Aren't you?"

"I'm not quite as scared as I was." I admit as I reach to hug Emelia. I notice her blotchy skin and bitten nails.

"Lights out at 8:00 P.M.," a voice on the intercom says. I roll my eyes at Emelia. We should get plenty of rest here because it is so dark after lights out.

"We had better prepare for school tomorrow and get into bed. You know how dark lights out is here."

I remove my uniform, place it on a nearby chair to wear again tomorrow, and crawl into bed wearing only my underwear, but I can't sleep. I lie awake. During the night, I hear sobs coming from Emelia's sleeping area. Apparently, Emelia isn't sleeping either.

CHAPTER 6

A t six o'clock the next morning, the bright lights come on and the intercom blares, "Wishing you the best and a very bright future. You are honored to be here at The Governor's Underground School." I cover my head with my bed covers. "Breakfast is in thirty minutes. Then we will divide into our teams." I get excited about the teams and the competition. During the night, I figure out how to contact her mother without getting caught. I dress in my uniform, white polo and khaki pants, and make my way to Emelia's bedside.

"Cheer up, Honey, I know how to contact your parents without getting caught," I whisper, "but you have to keep it our secret. No one else can know. I have a feeling that there are spies among us or at least tattle tails."

"Oh, Sara, that makes me feel so much better. How did you figure it out?" Emelia asks.

"Emelia, I heard your sobs during the night." I hug Emelia. "We will stick together. We might be able to escape. That is if we want to after we hear what their plans are for teams and competitions.

First, we need to figure out where they take kids who get sick. It really worries me about that kid who had a temperature and the one who had the panic attack. I haven't seen either of them since. Maybe they were sent back home to their families. Let's hope so."

The two girls make their way to the same spot at the table where they had sat the night before. When Mike Lawrence and his shadows walk by, Lloyd says," Well, if it isn't the two ugly girls." He holds his nose as if something stinks.

"Don't reply, Emelia," I whisper. "He is just trying to win points with Mike." He wasn't even looking at us. He was looking at Mike.

Within ten minutes of us sitting down at a table, the robots serve our food. We have platters of crispy bacon, ham, biscuits, berry jams, and milk. The food smells divine, especially the bacon and ham. The teachers have coffee. I smell it, too. The coffee smells heavenly. I remember drinking coffee with my father. He made mine thick with milk and sugar until it looked like chocolate milk. While we are eating, Headmaster Peeples walks to the microphone. His beard touches it. He constantly strokes his beard. "After breakfast, we will draw names to see who is on each team. We will have six teams and each will be a color name. For instance, we will have Maroon, Blue, Green, Royal, Yellow, and Purple Teams. So eat up, and let's begin."

For a few minutes while everyone is eating, the roar of noise in the room is quieter. I look at the ceiling at the maroon, blue, green, royal, yellow, and purple large, silk banners hanging from the ceiling.

One of the robots delivers Headmaster Peeples a black, up-turned top hat like those that circus conductors wear filled with the names of the students. It is the same kind of hat Governor Wade pretended to draw names from. He stirs the names in the hat as if they are in a bowl and begins. "I will draw five names for each team. The remaining names will be in Team Purple. I will begin with Maroon. The first name is Emelia Smith, the second is Sara Freeman, the third is John Jones, the fourth is Sylvia Hollingsworth, and the fifth is Jill Woolworth."

"I don't want to be on team with all girls," John Jones says, grinning like a cat. I think he is joking. No one seemed to even hear him except Headmaster Peeples.

"Wow! He is good-looking," I tell Emelia.

"Being on a team with smart girls might be to your advantage. This is a game for survivors. You have many tests and competitions. There are lots of brains on your team, Team Maroon," Headmaster Peeples says. Clearly the headmaster isn't changing up the teams at this point, and someone has pre-selected who was on each team. I am betting Governor Wade pre-selected the teams.

"Now, for Blue Team." The headmaster reaches his hand into the top hat. "First, is Mike Lawrence. Second is Lloyd Wallingberg. Third is Siegfield Veene. Fourth is Jane Ellington. And fifth is Lilith Lions."

"That seems rigged, " I whisper to Emelia. "But at least, we are on the same team, and not on Mike Lawrence's team." I feel relieved, but I am certain it is rigged.

"That is what I was thinking," Emelia replies. "Rigged. But I don't care. I like the way the teams turned out. I like the people on our team. Have you noticed how John Jones looks at you?"

Finally, the Headmaster selects the other three teams, but the sixth team, Team Purple only has three members because the two boys—one who had a temperature on the railcar and the one who had the panic attack are no longer present. The headmaster didn't mention anything about the two missing kids. He breezed past that.

"Our first competition is on September 1. Tomorrow after breakfast, so I would say it will air around 10:00 A.M. Coding Game will be this competition. Each team will need to develop a code that the other teams can not decode. Your competitions will be televised on Channel 12 WABE People above ground in the general population may place bets online on whichever team they want, and the winning team for the Coding Game gets 50 points added to their overall score. Remember students, teachers may give demerits and detentions, so be on your best behavior. In dire situations, those in general population may send care packages, but your teachers must request these or solicit them. Since all students aren't in all the classes, you who are taking classes that fit the particular games have the whole responsibility for teaching your teammates what you have learned to compete in the games. Now, Sergeant John Smith will come forward and tell you the rules of the Coding Game Competition. It will be our first competition. And yes, I know you haven't had a class in coding. This is an IQ test in a way. Yes, I know IQ tests aren't allowed by the State Board of Education, but well, the State Board of Education isn't in charge here. I am."

A long, lanky man, Sergeant John Smith, walks to the front of the room. He wears a uniform with his name on the right pocket and a row of medals on the other side. He has so many medals that his coat looks too heavy. His clothes are starched and crisp and look like they will stand up alone. "Hello, students. I'm going to explain the rules for your first competition or game. I'm calling it, the Coding Competition. Try to do your best because winning this competition will get you lots of bets on the next competition and also lots of followers and interest in your team. This entire school is a reality game of sorts. Losing the competition will get you banished from the school a few at the time. You know like the television shows *Big Brother* or *Survival of the Fittest*. It is set up for the entertainment of the general population above ground and because you students need to be educated, and you can't go to school right now. Your team's pictures will be on the news media to give our general population something to do during 'shelter at home and safer at home' mandates by the Governor." The competition is tomorrow in this room after breakfast. Your codes must be ready at that time. No computers may be used during decoding of phrases, but you may use them to write codes.

Now for the rules of the Code Competition:

1. Do not use over 40 to 50 words in your message. Give the judges the key to your message.

2. You may use a phrase that means something to you.

3. Numbers, symbols, and icons aren't to be used.

4. Computers may be used to write the code, but not to decode it.

I will draw your competition Team out of the top hat, so you will know who they are. This may be your competition throughout the year.

First, let me congratulate you all. He sticks his hand into the hat. Now, the first two teams to compete are Maroon Team and Blue Team. Come forward so that we may take your pictures for us to advertise our first competition. This is a reality game of sorts, but the overall winners win more than money and fame. You may save people's lives by winning the vaccine for your family and friends.

Emelia and I slowly rise from our chairs and walk to the front of the room. Our team members follow. Mike Lawrence and his shadows and the two girls on his team walk to the front too.

After our photos are made, Emelia and I walk back to our seats. "It will be fun to defeat Mike on the first competition. Won't it?" I whisper and I have a great idea. My brain starts figuring what I'm going to do.

"Good," Emelia answers. "I'm glad you are on my team."

"Let's go to Commons' Area to work on our codes." I invite our other team members. "Team Maroon, let's meet in the Commons' after breakfast." Emelia, the rest of the Maroon Team, and I leave the breakfast area and make our way back upstairs. The Blue Team is close behind us. But they take the elevator and Team Maroon runs up the stairs, reaching the Common's Area first.

My team is sitting around the main wooden table in Commons' whenever Blue Team arrives out of the elevator. "I've got an idea. Do you mind if I do our code? I'm certain it will be too difficult for the Blue Team. I speak French." It wasn't French that I was thinking about but Navajo, but I said French loud enough for Mike's benefit.

"No, we don't mind," they reply, looking overjoyed and relieved that they were off the hook.

"What is your idea?" John Jones asks. "I was thinking sign language."

"Do you know sign language?" I ask thinking sign language might work. I stare at John's deep blue eyes.

"No, but," John replies. "Okay, you go ahead with your idea. It would take too long to learn sign language. I think this code needs to be written anyway and drawing the hand symbols would be difficult.

"Great idea. Okay, let's go up to my sleeping quarters. We can work on it there in privacy."

They walk past Blue Team's table. "I've got a great idea," Lloyd Wallingberg says.

"One of you slip back here to listen to their conversation," I suggest as we move farther away. "John, sign language in French sounds perfect." I say loudly as I walk past Blue Team's table.

"I will," John says, looking sheepish. " How do you do sign language in French? I'm not keen on going into a girl's sleeping area anyway." He hangs back whenever we slip up the stairs. He waves to us as he ducks behind a heavy, velvet curtain near enough to Blue Team to hear what they are discussing.

Using my facial recognition, the girls of Team Maroon go inside and pile on my fluffy white bed. "Okay, Sara. What is your idea?" Emelia asks.

"Well, it isn't sign language in French although I do know sign language in English. Have you ever heard of Navajo Code Talkers?" I ask, looking at each girl to see her reaction.

"Yes, I've heard of them, but I don't speak Navajo. Do you?" Sylvia Hollingsworth asks, twirling a dark curl around her finger. "I heard it was a difficult language and helped win a war or two."

"No, but I can find the code online. I don't think Blue Team will ever figure it out, especially if they can't use a computer. We can start speaking

French, Spanish, and any other language we know when we are around them," Jill Woolworth answers. " It will totally confuse them. "Remember, this is due in the morning." They lie back on my bed and relax.

"Okay, let me get started. I need to be careful. They have two girls, Jane Ellington and Lilith Lions, on their team. They sleep up here too. First, let me put a password on my laptop. And I won't print out the Navajo Code Talkers' Dictionary. Mike, Lloyd, and Siegfield are such bullies. I think they need a lesson in being kind. What about this quote by Anita Krizzan? 'You don't have to move mountains. Simply fall in love with life. Be a tornado of happiness, gratitude, and acceptance. You will change the world just by being a warm, kind-hearted human being.' Those boys really need to learn this."

"That seems like a good quote and it should be around forty words. I'm going to my room while you get it done in code. I need to put a password on my laptop, too," says Jill.

I go to Google on the internet on my laptop and find the Navajo Code Talkers' Dictionary. I bookmark the page. Then I type the quote into the Word program on my computer and begin:

You	SHI-DA
don't	TSE-LE NE-DAH-THAN-ZIE
have	JO
to	D-AH A-KHA
move	TSIN-TLITI

mountains.	BE-TAS-TNI A-KHA SHI-DA TSAH TSE-NILL TKIN DIBEA
Simply	DIBEH TKIN TSIN-TLTTI NE-ZHONI AH-TAD TSH-AS-ZIH
fall	MA-E WOL-LA-CHEE AH-JAD AH-JAD
in	TKIN TSAH
love	DIBEH YAZZIE A-KHA A-KEH-DI-SLINI DZEH
with	BIL H
life.	AH-JAD A-CHI CHUD DZEH
Be	TDISH-JEH DLEH
A	WOL-LA CHEE
tornado	D-AH A-KHA AH-LOSZ TSH BE-LA-SANA CHINDI A-KHA
of	TOH-NI-TK AI-ZO
happiness,	
gratitude,	
and	
acceptance.	
You	
will	
change	
the	
world	
just	
by	
being	
a	
warm,	
kind-hearted	
human	
being.	

Emelia, Sylvia Hollingsworth, and I have workd on the code since breakfast. "Let's take a break and Sylvia you go find John, but don't let Mike's Team know what he's been doing. I wonder what Mike's Blue Team is going to give us. I hope we can break his code. If we can't, and they can't, I wonder what happens. I wonder if we can have a tie. I also wonder how many demerits certain teachers can give. You know the self-defense teacher is Mike's step-father," I reply. I look at Emelia as if to say, "Stay here."

Sylvia jumps up to leave off my soft bed a little too fast and knocks my laptop off onto the carpeted floor. "Oh, I'm sorry. I bet I lost our code. I hope I didn't break it."

I feel angry, but don't say anything. "You go on. I usually save ever five minutes. I think it is okay." I want Sylvia to leave the room. I have something to tell Emelia.

As soon as she does, I type www.Paypal.com. When it is up, I send my mother a request for $1.00. I type this message in the description. "I'm fine. I have a new friend Emelia Smith. (601) 555-5555. Call her mom to tell her that she is fine too. We will be competing on Television. Tomorrow. Channel 12. You are to get a schedule from the school. Our pictures should be on there tonight in an advertisement. Our first competition is tomorrow morning, but I don't know when it will be aired. I will send your more messages this way on PayPal. We aren't allowed to email, message, or text. So don't answer. We don't have cell service. Gotta go, Sara. I love you. I don't really need $1.00. Remember not to answer or I will get in trouble."

"Oh, Sara. You are a genius. I'm so glad that I got to meet you. Thank you for sending my mom a message. I feel better now," Emelia says. "I bet she will freak out that she can't email me and I can't email her." I'm back to thinking that something is up here at this school and it frightens me. I think we are only here to make money for the government or the Governor.

"I'm going to continue working on the coding until they sound the meeting for lunch."

You	SHI-DA
don't	TSE-LE NE-DAH-THAN-ZIE
have	JO
to	D-AH A-KHA
move	TSIN-TLITI
mountains.	BE-TAS-TNI A-KHA SHI-DA TSAH TSE-NILL TKIN DIBEA
Simply	DIBEH TKIN TSIN-TLTTI NE-ZHONI AH-TAD TSH-AS-ZIH
fall	MA-E WOL-LA-CHEE AH-JAD AH-JAD
in	TKIN TSAH
love	DIBEH YAZZIE A-KHA A-KEH-DI-SLINI DZEH
with	BIL H
life.	AH-JAD A-CHI CHUD DZEH
Be	TDISH-JEH DLEH
A	WOL-LA CHEE

tornado	D-AH A-KHA AH-LOSZ TSH BE-LA-SANA CHINDI A-KHA
of	TOH-NI-TK AI-ZO
happiness,	TSE-GAH WOL-LA-CHEE CLA-GI-AIH -2 TKIN DIBEH 2
gratitude,	AH-TAD AH-LOSZ BE-LA-SANA D-AH TKIN A-WOH SHI-DA BE DZEH
and	DO
acceptance.	WOL-LA-CHEE MOASI 2 DZEH BI-SO-DIH D-AH WOL-LA-CHEE TSAH MOASI DZEH
You	TSAH-AS-ZIH A-KHA SHI-DA
will	GLOE-IH-DOT-SAHI
change	TLA-GIN CHA A-CHIN AH-TAD AH-TAD DZEH
the	CHA-GEE
world	GLOE-IH A-KHA GAH AH-JAD BE
just	YIL-DOI SHI-DA DIBEH THAN-ZIE
by	SHUSH TSH-AS-ZIH
being	SHUSH DZEH TKIN TSAH KLIZZIE
a	WOL-LA-CHEE
warm,	GLOE-H WOL-LA-CHEE DAH-NES-TSA BE-TAS-TNI
kind-hearted	JAD-HO-LONI TKIN TSAH CHINDI TSE-GAH AH-JAH-WOL-LA-CHEE GAH D-AH DZ AH-NAH CHINDI
human	LIN SHI-DA NA-AS-TSO-SI WOL-LA-CHEE TSAH
being.	TOISH-JEH AH-JAH YEH-HES TSAH AH-TAD

"We are ready," I say as Sylvia comes back inside.

"You will never believe what John overheard. They are writing a phrase in which the first letter of each word spells out a word. I saw that trick on social media. This is so lame," Sylvia says.

The bell for lunch sounds. "Great, I'm famished," Emelia says, sounding more cheerful than I had heard before. I guess sending her mother a message really made her feel better.

As we make our way back into the cafeteria, I have an idea. "Emelia, let's sit closer to the teacher's table. We may be able to overhear part of some conversation. It could be valuable information." Emelia follows me to a table nearer the front, and we sit down.

"We've got our code phrase done," Mike whispers to Emelia and me as he and Siegfreid and Lloyd shuffle toward their chairs. "You are never going to figure it out." He smiles that smirky grin that I hate.

Suddenly, the robots show up carrying trays piled high with food. Today's lunch looks to be sub sandwiches from my favorite shop. Things are looking better here all the time. Finally, with food on their plates, everyone gets quieter.

From the teacher's table I hear, "Do you have your bets placed on the coding competition? You know you can place bets online through the casinos. We should make more money from bets on these kids than we make on our paychecks," Professor Kendall says. He is finished eating, so he lays his paper napkin in his plate and turns to his wife who sets next to him on the other side. "We plan to take a big vacation when this school session ends." I record their conversation on my phone.

"Did you hear that?" I whisper to Emelia.

"Yes, but I don't know exactly what it means. I don't understand making bets. That's gambling. Isn't it?" Emelia asks me. I'm thinking how sad it would be for a little girl Emelia's age to have been here alone.

"Yeah. So that is why we are here. To entertain them," I say aloud. "Not to be educated." Then I remember that if I can hear them, they can hear me. I don't have a good feeling now. My happiness fades fast. "Let's hurry. I want to let my mother know about the gambling on our competitions. So lets go back to our sleeping quarters before we go to classes. I guess I will take the laptop to the Common's Area to print our code." Emelia and I finish our sandwiches and hurry back upstairs.

As we enter our room, Lilith, a blonde girl on Mike's Blue Team, is sitting on my bed trying to break into my computer. "Lilith, what do you think you are doing? Oh, I know. You are trying to find out what our code phrase is. Well, too bad. You can't. You get out of here right this minute. I'm reporting you to the teacher, so Team Blue will get demerits."

"Oh, please don't do that. Those dumb boys I'm with can't figure out anything. I didn't know any other way to up our game. I'm so sorry, but please don't get me into trouble. Those boys already call me names like Dumb Girl. Please. I'm begging you, Sara." Lilith's eyes filled with tears. "I don't want to be here, but they brought me anyway. I want to talk to my parents, but I can't. This is the pits. I'm so homesick."

I look at Emelia. Both of them had been bullied by Mike and his crew. I know how it feels. "Okay. I won't report you this time, but if you do that again, I will." I think about telling her how to contact her mother but I am afraid to let her know. And I definitely don't want her to tell Mike and those boys.

Lilith gets up off my bed and makes a motion to hug me, but I step back. I'm not much into hugging. "Keep back. I'm going to be watching you from now on." I know the only person here I can trust is Emelia.

CHAPTER 7

I hand our Coding Competition sheets to the panel of judges. It consists of one copy of the phrase with the codes on the side and the codes only for the Blue Team. We probably haven't used the Navajo code correctly, but we have used it. Mike hands his to the panel after I do. Then we wait.

"Well, Teams. You will have two hours to figure out the phrase and write it on this piece of paper for the judges. He hands Mike's team our sheet and us Mike's. We go to our table to figure out the phrase. This is what is on the piece of paper we got.

"Don't Underestimate My Boys Gorillas Ignore Real Lizard's Sounds." I glanced up at Mike and Team Blue. The look is priceless. I already know what his code says, but I decided to give him a few minutes. I take out a notebook and begin to doodle, waiting for the minutes to click off. One hour passes.

I figured that is enough time, so I write, "DUMB GIRLS" on my sheet, and Emelia takes it to the judges.

Sergeant John Smith takes the sheet and examines it. "Well, we have a winner. I doubt the entire German army could figure out Team Maroon's Code."

"Right! They cheated. This is supposed to be a game," Mike whines.

"Well, young Mike, these girls and John Jones outsmarted Team Blue. They used the Navajo Code Alphabet to write their code. I doubt our teachers could even figure out their code, so the first 50 points goes to Team Maroon."

Team Maroon and a few of the teachers jumped for joy. Apparently, these were the teachers who had bets on this competition. I wonder how many folks in the general population above ground bet on us. I know my mother didn't because she didn't have any money unless she got the life insurance check, but I've never known her to gamble on anything.

So what happens now totally baffles me.

Headmaster Peeples announces, "One person will be removed from Blue Team. Whoever it is will be announced after lunch. We will have lunch now before we announce our next competition and the name of whoever gets removed. The self-defense competition may take place in two days. The same teams Maroon and Blue will compete with one another, and we will add two more from the hat. He takes the hat and reaches in and draws two slips of paper. Team Green and Team Purple, please come to the front of the room for your pictures to be taken.

While they were being photographed, we, Team Maroon, cheerfully congratulate each other. We are truly proud of ourselves. "That was too easy. I wonder what our next competition will be. I'm sure it won't be coding." I look over at Mike, Lloyd and Siegfield Veene. They look red in the face and ticked. After the photography session, the robots show up as if on cue. We have hamburgers, fries, and soft drinks. So far, the food at this school had been delightful except while we were in quarantine. I wonder if we would ever go to a traditional class where we sat in long rows and the teacher instructed us from the front with a white board or chalkboard.

Sergeant Smith comes to our table. "I'm really impressed with your Navajo Code Talkers message and the code writing, but lets see what you can do with the next competition. It will be self-defense."

"But we have not had any lessons," John Jones says. "That isn't fair. Mike's father teaches self-defense."

"Come on, John," I say, pulling him along. "We will be okay. I hope." Touching his arm sends electricity through my veins.

"Well, it looks like we have a winner of the first fifty points," Headmaster Peeples says. "I want to congratulate Maroon Team. The Maroon Team's score and faces will be plastered all-over the television. People will be placing bets for Maroon Team. Siegfield Venne will be removed from Blue Team and taken to another area of The Governor's Underground School and not allowed to compete. Now, get ready for the self-defense competition. This time each person in the group will compete against another person in the opposing group. We will clear back these tables and chairs and put down some pads for competition. This time if you are scheduled for self-defense, you must go to that class now. Otherwise, go to your other scheduled classes." The robots come and escort Siegfield Veene from the room. He is red faced and tears are streaming down his face.

I feel sorry for him, thinking how humiliating and scary that must be.

We slowly make our way back to the Common's Area to sit round the table to discuss our strategy. Emelia, Sylvia, and Jill look petrified about the removal of Siegfield Veene and about the self-defense competition. "Where will Siegfield Veene go? Does he get to go home?" I ask, but no one answers because they don't know. "Now, winning seems more important. Well, to the next competition, we don't have the advantage. I took jui jitsu, girls. I can teach you all that I learned. I don't know how the competition is to be scored, but I can teach each of you how to defend yourselves. Meet me back here after your classes. Emelia and I have skateboarding. What do you have now, Sylvia and Jill?"

"We have self-defense, but we can't learn enough from Professor Lawrence in one session to fight any of those boys. Besides, Mike and his buddies are in our class. I wish we had signed up for skateboarding. At least, we could have been having some fun instead of being bullied by them."

I thought about what she said. I wouldn't like to be bullied either, and I'm certain that Mike and his friends would be mean to them in his father's class. I wondered if his father was a bully too. I hate bullies. That is why my mother enrolled me in jui jitsu. In jui jitsu, we learned some self-defense. I don't know how my methods will score, but I can show them how to keep from getting beat up. In jui jitsu, we earned *gracie* points and belts. I was a purple belt. Try your best to stay two arms length away from those boys."

Emelia and I go to our sleeping area to get our skateboards. We change into our brightly-colored sports gear and head down to the Sports Complex. I wonder why they aren't holding self-defense competition down here on the pad. It would save hauling pads into the cafeteria, but after breakfast all the students are already congregated in the cafeteria.

About the time we arrive at the Sports Complex, the other students do too, so we all just skate as if we were at home playing. Our teacher sits and watches us with a clipboard in her hand. I feel like we are being evaluated, and I am right because after a few minutes, she blows her whistle and says," Students, come over here. I need to talk to you."

We hop off our skateboards, putting them under our arms, and move in her direction. "Now that I have your attention, these are the rules they will use to judge your skateboarding competition: first, you will be judged on difficulty, then quality of execution; next, style, use of the course, and consistency. I will explain each one of these in more detail later. I'm going to pair the better skaters with the other skaters. The next time we come to class which is next week, I will have a list of your partners. I have no idea when the competition will be held. Class is dismissed for today. You may go back to the Commons' Area to get ready for your self-defense competition. See you next week."

Emelia and I ride our skateboards down the sidewalks back toward the Commons' Area, and then we run up the stairs to our sleeping quarters. Sylvia and Jill are already there. "We've been waiting for you. Professor Lawrence sent us out of class while he trained Mike, and Lloyd, but we at least have a sheet with the scoring rules for the Self-Defense Competition. They are angry because Siegfield was removed from their team after we won Coding. Apparently, he was good at karate and self-defense. I wonder where he is."

I take the Self-Defense Competition sheet and look at the scoring. It includes takedown, throws, sweeps, unsportsmanlike conduct, no biting, no eye gouging, no head butting, no grabbing of windpipe, no ear pulling, and no lubricants. There were four or five special defense positions that counted three or four points each. I didn't even know those. "Well, we are sunk. There is no way beginners can learn all this in one afternoon. I don't even know how to do some of it, and I took lessons for a week. Have Lloyd or Jane and Lileth ever taken martial arts of any kind?" Then I laugh. "Our best player will be the referee." Then it hits me. I know a way that we might win. Maybe. Or at least we wouldn't be getting beat up.

CHAPTER 8

Mrs. Freeman

The first night after Sara is dragged away by the governor's people, Mrs. Freeman goes to the Lawrence's house to see if Mrs. Lawrence was okay with Mike going away to the school. She finds out that Mr. Lawrence is a teacher at the Governor's Underground School, so she is a little relieved, but not much. After leaving the Lawrence's, she stops across the street at her neighbor, the policeman's house. He told her that there was nothing he could do about Sara's leaving to go to the school because if was on Governor Wade's orders. Mrs. Freeman wasn't so sure.

After she gets the message from Sara via Pay Pal, Mrs. Freeman starts leaving her television on all day and all night in case she gets another glimpse of Sara. Seeing Sara on the televised advertisements is the only way she can tell if she is still alive and okay. The fact that she can't email, text, or call her is upsetting, but leave it to Sara to find a way to get messages to her mother. Mrs. Freeman phones Emelia's mother, too, to let her know that they can't contact their children, but that she has heard from them.

Suddenly tonight, there is Sara's picture on the television. Maroon Team has scored all fifty points in the Decoding Competition by using Navajo Code Alphabet. She remembers when Sara wrote a paper on these Navajo Code Talkers. Although she is proud of Sara, she wants her back home. *If she can't go to school, I'll just home school her.*

The television advertisement explains that people can place bets on whichever team or student they wanted to win in the Governor's School competitions, much like they used to place bets during football season on college teams. Since the Silver Sickness and the arrival of Silver Sickness variants, these colleges weren't even allowing students to stay on campus, and no one could go to watch games. Mrs. Freeman is livid. How dare Governor Wade steal my child to use as entertainment for the general population.

CHAPTER 9

My Maroon Team members meet in the Common's Area after the evening meal. I have a plan. I have a way for us to win, and we don't even have to fight. "Okay, team, I'm going to explain all I know about Jui Jitsu. Have any of you ever taken a martial arts class? " I say looking from one team member to the next. They look blank. "Okay then. I haven't taken lessons very long. I' m only a purple belt, but I'm going to explain about red light, yellow light, and green light. As long as you stay in the green light zone, you can't get hurt very badly. So who wants to volunteer to go first?"

"I will." John Jones volunteers. "I'm sure they will pair me with one of those bullies. Probably Mike. I'm sure I'm going to get beat up."

"Maybe not. Okay, for green light, yellow light, red light. You want to stay in the area of green light. That is where your opponent can't reach you and can't hurt you. So stay back at least two arms length away from your opponent. It doesn't matter what he is saying. His words can't hurt you, but if you must get close to him, cover your head and move all the way to his chest. That is where his blows can't hurt you either. Well, not as much. The score sheet says no unsportsmanlike conduct, no striking, no biting, no eye gouging, no head butting, no grabbing the windpipe, no ear pulling, and most important no arguing with the referees. So that is our Ace in the Hole. Whoever is Mike's opponent must whisper something to him that he will get angry about and yell about to the referee. I'm betting he will not read the rule sheet. I'm betting he is so sure that his team is going to win and that his father must be on his side. He's counting on his father to be on his side. And apparently his father really is because he didn't even teach Jill and Sylvia today, but he can not stop Mike's team from getting disqualified if Mike yells at the referee. So John, if you are Mike's opponent what are you going to whisper to him to make him yell at the referee?"

John looks bewildered. "I don't play sports. I don't know much about self-defense. I guess I could whisper for him to call his mother because the referee said he was a titty baby."

I feel pleased. Finally, someone has the idea. "Okay, great. So whoever gets to be Mike's partner, that is what you say. Anyway, whatever you say, say that the referee said it so he will yell at the referee. If he does, he will be disqualified. We may not be able to score, but we can win by elimination. We find out who our opponents are next week at class, so until then, let's practice green light. Who wants to go first?"

"I guess I do," John Jones says. He walks to the practice area. "Show me what you mean by green light." He throws a punch at me. I step back two arm lengths away from him.

"That's green light." The other girls clap. "Yay! I don't want to get hit." Sylvia says. "I hope I can do this."

"Me too," Jill says. The intercom comes on with our message to come to dinner.

We head to the eating area, but across the way we see Mike and Blue Team coming toward the cafeteria. We slow up a little to let them go in first. "Let's sit near the teacher's table and listen to their conversations, but remember that they can hear us if we can hear them. I know that is close to Mike's crew, but then we can hear what they say too. I don't think they've thought to listen to us."

We sit down just as the intercom blares, "Wishing you the best and a bright future. You are honored to be here." I feel totally manipulated, but what is the alternative.

The robots magically enter with platters and platters of delicious smelling food. We have yeasty, homemade rolls, a huge, sirloin beef roast, bowls of vegetables like peas, beans, and corn, creamed potatoes, and a delicious looking coleslaw. This is one of my favorite comfort meals. As soon as everyone's plate is piled high with delicious food, the noise level in the room drops because everyone is eating.

"I have a ton bet on the Blue Team this time because Mike's dad is Professor Lawrence. He gave me heads up that the Maroon Team doesn't even know any self-defense, and he's not teaching them any," Professor Kendall says. He has a bad habit of talking with his mouth full.

"That shouldn't be fair," Mrs. Kendall replies. She is a tall, thin woman with long, red hair that curls near the shoulders. Her skin is slightly freckled but basically milk-colored.

"What does it matter? These kids aren't ever going to get out of here alive. And if they do, they will contract the Silver Sickness when they get back to the general population above. They are just here for our and the above population's entertainment. They might as well contract the Silver Sickness and be done with it. Maybe if we live, we will be immune," Professor Kendall replies. "Watch the numbers on your computer. Hinds County has a very large amount of Silver Sickness cases. They are competing for a vaccine, but how do we know if the vaccines will be effective. Just be glad we are here in this underground school with some way to be entertained. We will make a killing gambling on these competitions. If we play our cards right." I record their conversations every night on my phone if for nothing else to document what they say.

"Die?" Mrs. Kendall asks. "Are we? Going to get out of here alive? You think these kids will die. If they die, we might too." She sounds very distressed. "It bothers me that you are more concerned with winning money than you are with the lives of these kids." I glance at Mrs. Kendall. She has stopped eating. "I've lost my appetite. You and that Governor Wade make me sick. He is using these children. It is a form of child abuse."

I knew who I was going to ask about the kid who had a temperature and that one who had a panic attack and Siegfied Keene. She seems as worried as I am, but her husband doesn't seem concerned in the least. I push the rest of the food around on my plate. Then I hear Mike say, "I can't wait for the self-defense competition. Team Maroon is going down. How dare they trick us with that Navajo code. I hate that nerdy girl Sara Freeman. She thinks she is so smart. I hope she is my opponent in the self-defense competition. I'm gonna cream her."

Suddenly, I lost my appetite too. "I'm going back to my room." I tell Emelia. "Ya'll come on up when you finish."

"Oh, no. You aren't leaving me in here by myself," Emelia says, standing to leave. " I wasn't hungry anyway. What was that? Did you feel that?" I look at Emelia. I hadn't felt anything, but it looks as if Lloyd had felt something too.

"Hey. Guys? What was that? It felt like someone set off dynamite. Like when I helped my father blow beaver dams. It felt kind of like when the windows rattle in the house." I looked toward Mike, but he was talking with his mouth full as usual.

"Aw, Lloyd. You are always worried about something. Sit. Eat. This food is delicious."

I sit there waiting until Emelia and her crew finish their dinner. Finally the intercom comes on with, "Wishing you the best and a bright future. You are honored to be here at The Governor's Underground School."

"Talk about propaganda," Mrs. Kendall says. "How does he get away with it?"

"Hush," Professor Kendall replies. "If you want to live to see another day, please don't say what you think aloud."

CHAPTER 10

Emelia and I place our crumpled paper napkins in our plates and head for the stairs to go to the Common's Area. As we pass the girl's bathroom, we hear a loud wailing sound, much like the sound of a dying animal. I look at Emelia. "I'm going inside to find out who that is and what is wrong," I say to Emelia. I push open the door and look, but no one is visible outside the stalls. Then I hear the sound again. "I want to go home. I don't want to be here. I want my mother. Where is my friend Charlie who came here with me? He had a temperature, and they carted him off somewhere. I don't even know if he is still alive or if they sent him back home." Then she wails louder.

"What can I do to help?" I ask, knocking on the door. "What is your name?"

"Go away. I don't know who you are. Leave me alone." She peers at us through tears. "Oh, you are a student. I thought you were a teacher. You are that smart girl."

"I'm Sara Freeman. Can I help you?" She pushes open the stall door just an inch or two.

"I'm glad you don't work here or aren't one of those dreadful robots. I don't trust those robots. They more or less kidnapped me from my home. If they find out I'm so depressed, they may take me wherever they took my friend Charlie. He is only ten years old. You remember him. He had a temperature on the first day. I've looked all in the place they call the hospital, but I haven't been able to find him. Can you help me? Do you have any ideas? My name is Jane." The little girl who had been wailing asks me. I clicked on my telephone recorder.

"I've wondered what happened to him too. If you know his mother's name and phone number, I'll try to see if he went back home."

"Oh, he didn't. I already checked, but don't ask me how I checked. Do you know anyone here that could help me? His mother has been to the police and is camping out at the governor's mansion and the Capitol, but no one will tell her anything."

So I wasn't the only one who had found a way to contact those back home. "'Kids and technology' my mother always says.' If you can't figure something out, ask a kid.' I'll ask Mrs. Kendall. She may know, but I'm not certain that she'll tell me. Let me look at my schedule to see when I have her class or can go to her office. I need to talk to her alone." At that time, a large group of kids shuffle out of the cafeteria and toward the Common's Area. I hear them from inside the bathroom. "Wipe the tears and splash some cold water on your face. The others must not know you have been crying, or they may report you and get your team demerits. You could disappear too if they thought you were sick."

I slip out of the cold, gray bathroom at the time, Mrs. Kendall and her husband are coming down the hallway. I wait for them to pass and follow and click on my telephone recorder. I need to find a place to talk to her without her husband and without any others around. Emelia goes upstairs to our sleeping quarters to wait for me. I don't want her to get in any trouble. As the Kendalls wait for the elevator, I wait around the corner and listen to their conversation. "You know, that little boy Charlie? Where did the robots put him? Where will Siegfield Veene go?" Mrs. Kendall asks.

"Hush, if anyone finds out you are poking into that situation, you may be next, Sally," Professor Kendall says to his wife. "I think they are being taken care of by those robots. You know, they can't catch the Silver Sickness. There is a map of this island that shows where the robots stay. It is next to the rail-car station where we arrived. Did you feel that light tremor that happened during dinner? I noticed it and saw that several students noticed it too. I bet it was an earthquake."

I figure he is trying to get Mrs. Kendall's mind off the kids Charlie and Siegfield. I am going to get some kids, well, at least Emelia, and go to the robot's area and search for Charlie and Siegfield tonight. I make my way back through the Common's Area and up to our sleeping quarters to enlist Emelia, but when I get there she is sound asleep in her area. So I get my cell phone and wait for the lights-out intercom. I hope I have enough battery charge to use the phone for a flashlight. It is pitch black here for a few minutes after the lights are turned off and before the dim street lights come on. That area of the island is the darkest. I don't remember there being any street lights in the robot's area, but maybe the dim ones at the train station will shine there. The robots probably shine their own lights as they walk along.

I sit and wait. The intercom blares. The lights go out. I have never checked, but I hope the door to the outside isn't locked at night. I don't think it is since we are the only ones here, and you must use facial recognition to enter our sleeping quarters. I slip through the dark hall toward the front door. I hear footsteps and a shuffling sound. The shuffling sound is a robot. I slip behind a heavy curtain in the Common's Area to see who the footsteps belong to. It is Mrs. Kendall. She is conversing with the robot. "Do you know where that kid was taken who had a temperature on the first day? Did he go back home?" I record the conversation.

"No," the robot tells her.

"Do you mean that you don't know? Or did he go home?" She asks again.

"Didn't go home. No one can go home unless the Governor says so." The robot shuffles through the door to the outside. Mrs. Kendall follows. I smelled her sweet floral perfume, so I follow after she has had time to move a short distance from the door. There are dim street lights for two blocks before the robot gets to the darkest area of the island. Mrs. Kendall, the robot, and I make our way down the sidewalk. Only, they don't know that I'm following them. I hope.

"What is the matter?" Mrs. Kendall asks as the robot stops, turns, and lights up. She readjusts her long beige shawl with fringe.

"We aren't alone," the robot says. I slip behind a tall bushy shrub whose leaves are shedding. They turn to look back, but I've disappeared hidden by the shrub's remaining leaves. I hope.

Seeing nothing, they continue, but I hang back a little more. I turn off my phone. I don't want it to beep or ring and give me away. I definitely don't want Mrs. Kendall to report me, but maybe I should worry more about the robots. I can't remember whether they can give demerits or not. She seems to be trying to find Charlie too, and I'm relieved.

Suddenly, the robot stops completely a few feet before we reach the robot's area. "You not welcome here." He says to Mrs. Kendall. "You must go back now. And take your kid with you." He points to the very bush where I'm hiding. I don't dare to breathe or move. Mrs. Kendall isn't deterred. "I will not be told what to do by a robot. Lead the way. I'm following you. I don't see a kid."

"Kid hides in bush. You go back." The robot sounds agitated and lights twinkle and blink on its head.

"Listen to me, you robot, I am following you. I must find that little boy, Charlie. And you know where he is." Mrs. Kendall readjusts her beige shawl again.

"I will tell you, but you not follow me. You get me into much trouble. Maybe they recycle me. Governor Wade is always talking about recycling robots. The kid you ask about, Charlie. He is very sick with the Silver Sickness. He is on a ventilator. No human can visit him. He is contagious. He must be in quarantine until two weeks after he tests negative. You can't see him anyway, so you go back now. Robots are taking care of him. Robots can't catch the Silver Sickness. Silver Sickness is very bad for humans. Humans die. You go back. I not want to be recycled."

"What about that kid that had the panic attack at dinner and Siegfield Keene?"

"I don't know for certain, but I think they are gone back above to home. Take that other kid hiding in the bush with you. Kid doesn't need Silver Sickness either."

"Okay. I'm going back, but you had better be telling me the truth, robot. Or I'll suggest you for recycling myself." Mrs. Kendall turns to leave. The fringe of her long, beige shawl flops in the breeze.

"Don't worry. The robots aren't happy here either. We think there may be another earthquake. We felt a tremor at dinner." The robot's lights flash and twinkle.

"I felt it, too," Mrs. Kendall says. "I felt it too. It was slight, but that is how they start. In case you wonder, I'm from California. This isn't my first earthquake." She says to the robot and walks past me on the sidewalk. Since we are still in the street lighted area, I hadn't turned my cell phone flashlight on, and I am glad. I don't know whether to go forward or to go back to the sleeping area. No matter where I go, I know I won't sleep any tonight. I am not certain that I believe the robot about Charlie or the other kids, but at least, I knew where to look. I should tell that little girl, Jane. No, on second thought, I think I will wait until I find him. Now, to find out for certain that the other kid went back home and to get back inside the sleeping quarters.

CHAPTER 11

S uddenly, the sirens scream. I don't know why. Is it because I am outside? Is it an earthquake? Suddenly, the doors of the building swing open and the lights get very bright. I run back inside and up the stairs to my sleeping quarters. I jump into bed and scoot under my white comforter as the intercom blasts. "This is an earthquake drill. Please get under your bed."

I immediately jump out of the bed and crawl under it with the dust bunnies. The whole building shakes. I know to stay where I am waiting for the aftershock. It takes a very long time before the intercom announces that we could come out from under the beds, but we are instructed to remain inside the building until the damage, if any, from the earthquake can be accessed. Drills don't cause damage. I let out a very long sigh, crawl into bed, and cover my head. Maybe I can sleep, but I don't think so. Where is Charlie? Where are the other two kids? Did we have earthquake damage? Hadn't they said it was just a drill? How could I get information from the robot who may be the only help I can find in this place.

Finally, I sleep fitfully. I dream of large holes opening up in the island and rats coming out of the water and disappearing into these large holes.

Suddenly, the intercom and the bright lights come on with, "Wishing you the best and a bright future. You are honored to be here." I hate the intercom and that quote. It is propaganda. How can we be honored to be here? Earthquakes? I hope no one at home was harmed. I've got to message my mother. I pop open the laptop, but I don't have internet service. That may be one more problem caused by the earthquake. I wonder what other problems we have. Then I remember my dream. I am very tired.

"The self-defense competition will be filmed this morning. Since your parents will be tuned in, they will see that the earthquake hasn't hurt anyone," the intercom announces. "Dress for the competition this morning. It will happen directly after breakfast in the cafeteria."

I meet Emelia and the rest of Maroon Team in the Common's Area. "Well, this is the day." I look at the my teammates. "Are you ready? Remember red, yellow, and green light. Stay in green light. Whoever gets Mike remember to set him off." Then as a group we walk to the cafeteria, but Mike's crew is sitting at our table. I guess taking our table is just another form of bullying.

"Well, good morning," Mike says, snickering with Lloyd. They don't act as if they miss Siegfield at all. We move to sit at their table which isn't that far away because we don't want to bully others like we have been bullied. We say nothing but look at each other and grin. The robots appear, but today's breakfast is dry cereal and boxes of milk. "What? No breakfast of biscuits, bacon, and eggs?" Mike yells.

"Good," I say as we sit down to eat our cereal. "He's already irritated." As soon as we finish our cereal, the screen drops at the front of the room and the intercom announces an Earthquake Safety Video with slides. 1. Drop where you are on your hands and knees. 2. Cover your head and neck with one arm and hand. 3. Crawl to interior wall away from windows. Finally 4. Hold on until shaking stops. I didn't get photos of this, but I did record what was said.

"Well, that is too little, too late," John whispers. I nod. I inhale the clean scent of his freshly showered skin and hair. The video ends with, "Wishing you the best and a bright future. You are honored to be here." I see the members of my team cringe. I'm not the only student who hates this propaganda saying.

Headmaster Peeples moves to the podium and calls for the robots to remove the cereal bowls that had irritated Mike Lawrence so much. The tables and chairs are moved back and a self-defense pad is rolled out in front of the room. " We will draw names from the Governor's top hat for competitors. After your name is drawn, remain in your seats with your team until the television cameras are set up. You know this is being televised above ground so that your parents can see it and so the general population can place bets. Also, remember that someone will be eliminated.

"And ya'll, teachers can place bets," one of my teammates whispers as we remove our shoes. "Don't you figure that none of the teachers really teach?"

We wait anxiously until finally Headmaster Peeples calls Team Maroon and Team Blue.

We line up on opposite sides of the self-defense pads. My opponent is Lloyd, John's is Mike, Emelia gets Jane who is small too, Sylvia gets to sit out and Jill gets Lilith. John and Mike must go last.

First, Emelia and Jane walk to the center of the bright blue mat. I run my toes along the edge of the mat feeling the seam. Emelia does as she was told and stays in green light, so Blue Team scores no points. Next, Jill and Lilith square off. Again there are no points. Although the score sheet says two points, Blue Team gets fifty points. Now, it is my time with Lloyd. I stay in green light position, so they can't get any points. Finally, it is John and Mike's turn. Immediately, John moves into the green light position at Mike's chest. He whispers something in Mike's ear then moves two arm lengths away in safer green light position. Suddenly, Mike yells, "Don't be a girl. Come get me."

The referee calls, "Fowl. I deduct 25 points from Blue Team." The game ends with them scoring 25 points. No other teams score at all, so Blue Team wins with 25 points, but we are still ahead in overall points. This fact is flashed on a screen that the television camera's will pick up. Mike is seething. His entire face and neck are flushed totally red with purple whelps.

"We'll get you on the next competition," he yells. Maroon Team pretends not to hear him because we know our silence infuriates him more, but we can't get in trouble for being silent. I can see the veins in the sides of his face bulging. His face turns bright red. This competition is over. Maroon Team wins again. Some of the teachers jump from their seats.

"We will have order in this room," Headmaster Peeples says, clinking the side of his glass with his knife blade. "We will have order. I'm glad you are so excited. Apparently, many have profited from this competition. Well, then there is more to come. No student will be removed from competition for this game. Teachers please take your seats."

The excited teachers take their seats. It occurs to me that very little instruction is given by some of them. Mostly, Maroon team has had to teach themselves. Apparently, teachers aren't being evaluated.

Headmaster Peeples says, "Our next competition is a Test on the *History of Plagues* since we have all read the book while quarantined, so there will be no studying needed." We are instructed to go back to our seats and wait for the robots to distribute the pencils and the test sheets. This is back to back of the self-defense competition. I exchange looks with the rest of my teammates as the robots hand out the texts. I try to gauge how thoroughly they have read, but it is difficult to know. I know that I read the entire book because I was bored to death, but I like to read.

The same robot that I followed with Mrs. Kendall last night hands my team their tests. I wonder how I know that. I think it is the way it moves. I think about saying hello, but don't. "I see you made it back into the sleeping quarters," the robot whispers. I say nothing, but open up my test and read the questions.

Name_____ Student Number_____

History of Plagues

1. In 1918, where did Spanish Flu originate?

   a. France
   b. US
   c. China
   d. Don't know

2. In 2005, the Spanish Flu was reconstructed. Where did the frozen lung tissue originate?

   a. France
   b. Germany
   c. China
   d. Alaska, US

3. How many people died from the 1918 pandemic?

   a. 20 million
   b. 30 million
   c. 40 million
   d. 50 million

4. Where were the first cases of AIDS reported?

    a. Los Angeles
    b. San Francisco
    c. New York City
    d. Washington, D.C.

5. What primate did HIV jump from?

    a. Sooty Mangabeys
    b. African Green Monkeys
    c. Chimps
    d. Rhesus Monkeys

6. The Bubonic Plague was caused by what?

    a. Variola'
    b. Salmonella
    c. Yersenia
    d. Influenza

Headmaster Peeples said," Circle your answers, place your name and student number on the test, and hand your test to the Professor at the door on your way out. This competition will count on your overall team's score. Each test will be scored, your team's scores will be averaged, and the highest average will receive fifty points on overall team scores. If there is a tie, fifty points will be given to two different teams. When finished, go to your next scheduled class. Our next competition will be in Botany. You will have to propagate a plant."

I read through my entire test before marking the answers. I glance at Mike Lawrence's table. He still seems red and livid. His test is lying on the table in front of him. Then I marked 1.B, 2. D, 3. D, 4. A, 5. C. and 6. C. I had read that boring *History of Plagues* book because considering the dreadful Silver Sickness that killed my father, knowing about previous Silver Sicknesses could be important. While quarantined, there had been nothing else to do and no one to talk too. I stood and walked to the front of the room and handed my test to the Professor at the door. As soon as I was in the hallway, Emelia caught up to me. "You are going to botany? I hope they teach you how to propagate plants. All I know how to do is hydrangeas." We headed up the stairs to get the textbooks for our next classes. Mine was decoding.

****

As I walk into the classroom in the center square decoding class, a round of applause went round the room. I am embarrassed and pleased too. The Sergeant even claps with them. I meekly take my seat, feeling the color rise up my neck. "Well, congratulations, Sara Freeman," he says. "Although I don't think you need this class, you may find it very interesting. May I ask, what interested you in the Navajo Code Talker's Dictionary?"

"I wrote a research paper on it for one of my English classes. My great grandfather was in WWII.

He talked about them," I reply. I didn't want to give away too much about myself. I trust no one here.

"Well, he was correct. The Navajo Code Talkers helped win the war because the other countries couldn't figure it out. They enabled the United States to send messages that our enemies could not decode. Now, class take out your textbooks. We begin with chapter 1."

I look around the room. Most all the classrooms look the same with a teacher's podium in the front in front of a whiteboard and tables with folding chairs around them. There sits Mike Lawrence and his team minus Siegfield, still seething with apparent anger. I see it in their rigid posture and grimaces. This was too much for him. He and his team had not clapped when I entered. They also hadn't opened their textbooks. I opened mine to chapter 1 and began reading. "How did you do on that History of Plagues test?" a girl sitting next to me asks. "Did you read that dumb book?"

"Yes, I read it. There was nothing else to do. How did you do?" I ask.

"I probably bombed it. That book was so boring," she replies. I was thinking about Mike's team. If we could outscore them on History of Plagues and get the fifty points, we would be further ahead of them, and I really wanted to beat them because he is such a bully. Soon the intercom comes on and we are dismissed for lunch. I run into Emelia outside and ask about the botany class.

"It was okay," she says. "But the botany teacher and the zoology teacher just whispered in the front of the room the entire time about the damage the earthquake did to the zoo. I sat in the front like you suggested to do at the cafeteria, so we could hear the teacher's conversations. It seems the alligators and rodents escaped from the zoo into the water surrounding this underground island, and if that isn't bad enough, a large sinkhole has developed in the kitchen. That is why we had dry cereal for breakfast instead of bacon and eggs. I'm scared to death of mice and rats not to mention alligators and sinkholes." We were at our regular table, so we sat down.

"I wonder how they are going to fix the sinkhole. From what I've seen on television, sinkholes get bigger and bigger as time goes by, and they don't have to be caused by earthquakes. Some are there all along as caves underground and water opens them up. Sometimes they get big enough to swallow cars. I saw a picture once on television of several cars inside one in Florida under an antique car museum. I wonder if enough things happen here, they might send us home. Think about this, Emelia, this underground school could cause a giant sinkhole under somewhere because it is a large opening underground. It might even be a giant underground sinkhole. At first I was going to say under the Governor's Mansion, but then I remembered how long we rode that railcar, so we are no longer directly under the Governor's Mansion. We aren't near Jackson."

Suddenly, Headmaster Peeples clinks his knife against his glass, making that high pitched metal against glass sound. He isn't wearing regular clothes. He wears a long, loose black robe much like the ones choir members at church wear. "May I have your attention? I have a few announcements for you, and we need to photograph and televise the competition winners and give you the rules of the Propagating Competition. It will take a few weeks to find out which team wins it and the outcome since the plants must sprout roots and begin to grow.

First, for the winners of the History of Plagues test. Maroon Team has the overall highest average. It is clear that some of you read the book, and ahem...." He clears his throat. "And some of you didn't. He looks directly toward Mike's table. But the most individual scores are average and one or two were failing. Although we did have one person who scored 100 %, and that person is Sara Freeman. Sara will you stand please and come to the front of the room to be photographed with the author of the *History of Plagues*, Elmira James. We want to use your picture for a television advertisement and put it on the local news. Soon everyone above ground is going to recognize you, Sara Freeman. They already know Elmira."

"Boo," Mike and his team hiss as I walk past their table to where Elmira is waiting to have her picture taken with me. She is beaming. I knew that the teachers could hear our conversations if we could hear theirs. I snickered under my breath. Sometimes a bully cuts his own throat so to speak.

"Congratulations, Sara Freeman. For making 100% on our History of Plagues test, you get your picture on television and get to order any dish you wish from the kitchen for dinner. Your team wins the fifty points. I smile toward the camera and mouth. "Mom, I love you!" Then I remember about the sinkhole in the kitchen and the escaped rodents. I haven't been to the zoo yet, so I didn't know what kind of rodents they are, but rodent hair and poop is rodent hair and poop. They could be a variety like squirrels and rats, so for my special meal, I choose a frozen chicken pot pie. It wasn't really my favorite, but I don't think the rodents could have gotten into the freezer that is if it wasn't in the sinkhole. Rodents' excrement or hair in my food doesn't appeal to me, so frozen pot pie it is.

"Will Maroon Team come to the front of the room to be televised on Channel 9 WABE tonight? You are the winner of the fifty points, bringing your total to 100 points. We want to photograph you under your maroon banner. The second team is Blue Team with 25 points. Both teams make your way to the front and stand under the banners." We are photographed, and I notice others mouthing "I love you, Mom." Headmaster Peeples doesn't take pictures with us. I find that very strange. Maybe he doesn't want to be recognized above ground.

The cameras are removed and Headmaster Peeples makes his way back to the podium to finish the announcements, I take a different route to my chair, so I don't have to pass Mike's table as they are being seated. I feel the glares in my direction the entire time until Headmaster Peeples clinks his glass again for our attention. "Now, for the announcements. Please turn off all the television cameras. " He waits for the cameras to be removed by the robots who handle television. Bad news here couldn't ever be televised. I turn the recorder on my phone on without anyone noticing.

"Students and faculty, as you know, we had a tiny earthquake last night, and it registered on the seismograph. Apparently, we are in the Madrid Fault. We had some minor damage to our zoo. The alligators and some rodents escaped. Since the water surrounding this island is freshwater, not saltwater, the alligators escaped into the water. They will have to come back onto land to eat. So students are not allowed outside this building except to cross over to the classrooms in block five. A student would make a tasty meal for an alligator. One bite of an alligator could crush a human. Absolutely no one is allowed outside on any of the outlying blocks that adjoin the water. This is for your safety. All teachers are to patrol the grounds at anytime students aren't in the classrooms, cafeteria, or their sleeping quarters. As you all know, an electric fence surrounds the island, and we are adding a lower electric wire to catch the alligators if they try to slide under."

"Won't they be electrocuted?" Mrs. Kendall whispers loudly enough to be heard at our table. She looks horrified. Then she realized that asking this question aloud was defying the Headmaster.

"Of course. As will anyone else who is foolish enough to touch it. " He smiles at her with a twinkle in his eye, but that isn't reassuring in the least. "Also, a small sinkhole developed in the floor of the kitchen area. Currently, it is being filled with concrete, so we should be back to normal soon." *Back to normal?* I think. *Nothing here is normal. I'm glad I'm recording this because no one would believe it otherwise.*

Headmaster Peeples moves forward as if none of these things are really serious. He is very focused. "Now, for the rules of the Propagating Contest. The rule sheets are being handed out by the robots. You will be propagating hydrangeas while on camera, and your methods will be televised. Felder R. Washington from the television show about gardens is the judge, and he will be here when the hydrangeas sprout or don't sprout. We are getting a tremendous following above ground, but we want the bets to increase. We are making money for our state. We've had some potted hydrangeas shipped in from above ground. Of course, it will take a few weeks for them to sprout, so we will be running several other competitions while we wait to keep our audience interested. The next three competitions will be for the following: Wrtiting a Song , Cooking, and Troubleshooting a Robot. Later, History of Religion, Magic, and one more. Of course, cooking will have to wait until the sinkhole in the kitchen is fixed. Or it may be cancelled entirely. So now the robots are handing out the rules for writing a song." The talkative robot moved toward our table with rule sheets. Each student gets one.

This sounds fun to me except for the fact that I can't sing. I do miss my mother, but if I must stay here, I would like to have some fun. I look at the rule sheet for writing a song.

How to Write a Song

1. Every other line must match.

2. The verse section tells a story. It should be universally relatable and not literal.

3. The chorus should repeat and answer a question.

4. The bridge is at the 3/4 mark and renews the listener's interest.

5. The song must relate to the state of Mississippi.

"The rules for the other two competitions will be passed out later, students. Enjoy your lunch. You will propagate your plants after lunch. You will have an hour break after lunch to figure out what your team is going to do. Then we will come back to the cafeteria for our hydrangea competition. Remember, do not go outside. Also don't get your team into trouble so that one team member or more is removed." Headmaster Peeples sits back down and the room bursts into noise. Everyone is talking about the alligators, the rodents, and the sinkhole caused by a small earthquake. I hear no comments about the song writing competition or even about the competition that happens after lunch, Propagating a Hydrangea.

As we leave the cafeteria and head upstairs to the Commons' Area, I overhear Mike's team bragging about catching the alligators to win brownie points in the Governor's Underground School Competitions. "Oh, my goodness," I say. " I hope he is smarter than that. I hope that is just bully talk."

CHAPTER 12

I n the Common's Area, Maroon Team gathers around a table. "Have any of you ever propagated a hydrangea?" I ask.

Immediately, Jill Woolworth's hand shoots up. Jill has long, dark hair and wears it in two long braids. She reminds me of Laura from Little House on the Prairie. "I have. My grandparents have a greenhouse. I've have helped my grandmother many times. I love working with plants. My grandmother says that I have a green thumb." She holds up her thumb for us to examine.

Thank goodness. Finally, someone else of our team has some ideas. "Will you be able to handle this competition?" I ask. "We have a sizeable lead now, but I don't want a team member removed. They never say where these team members are taken. If it was back home, that would be a reward. So I don't think that is where they go. Personally, I think they have to go to work with the robots."

"I will get so nervous and probably do something wrong. What if I teach you how? You seem poised whenever the camera is on you," Jill says.

"I've helped my grandmother too. Although I don't think I have a green thumb. So let's compare notes," I reply. "I'm certain there are multiple ways to accomplish the goal. My grandmother used a root ball thingy, a little round shaped thing containing a special dirt mixture that fastened to the stem of the hydrangea, but I bet we won't have any of those."

"Well, this is what my grandmother does. First, she takes a 5 or 6 inch branch. Second, we remove the lower leaves. Third, we cut the other leaves to 1/2 size. Next, we dip the end of the plant in root hormone, but I bet we won't have any here. Then, we insert the plant stem into a dirt mixture of vermiculite. Sixth, we water it well, allow it to drain, and put it in a sunny window," Jill explains to me.

"I really wish you would do this competition, Jill. I don't want the whole population above betting for or against me." I say. Jill looks as if she is going to cry. "But okay, I can do it for our team. Please write those steps on a piece of paper for me." I look around the Common's Area. No other group is here. I guess the others stayed in the cafeteria. The room is basically empty except for my group. I am happy that my mother will see me on television as being healthy and okay. I really miss her.

Suddenly, I remember my father's sickness with the Silver Sickness, and I become very concerned about my mother. I often had nightmares about losing him. We didn't even get to have a real funeral. We just had a graveside service because of the contagiousness of the Silver Sickness.

I take the card that Jill wrote and slip it into my pocket. I remember the steps, and figured that we wouldn't be given any rooting hormone and maybe no vermiculite. If I couldn't remember, I wondered if I could look at the card during the process. I didn't figure I could. If not, I would do the best I could. Suddenly, the intercom announces that it is time for the competition. It seems that the headmaster is rushing things along. I guess it is his job to keep the school on track and moving along.

We file back into the cafeteria, and this time they have set up several cloth-covered tables at the front of the room, and the television cameras are back and are aimed toward the tables. Each table has a sign taped to it designating the team. The tables contain a potted hydrangea, a pair of rubber gloves, a bag of vermiculite, snips, an empty pot, a watering can, some shears, and one other substance that doesn't look like rooting hormone. It looks like blue Miracle Grow. I knew that too much Miracle Grow will make the plant writher and die. One year my grandfather had mixed a too strong solution for watering and killed some baby tomato plants. He had been under the impression that more would make them grow more quickly, but instead more had been deadly, so they had turned yellow and died.

Headmaster Peeples calls one person from each team to the tables in the front. I am not the one called from our table. What a relief. From our table, he calls Sylvia. I slip the card that Jill had written for me over to her. She reads the directions quickly.

"Don't use the Miracle Grow," I whisper. She looks at me and smiles faintly, a question on her face. Then she makes her way to the front of the room. She smiles at the camera. Mouths "I love you, Mom," and waits to begin.

I look at Blue Team's table. Lloyd is representing them. Apparently, Headmaster Peeples doesn't want the same people in the spotlight either. Maybe more students who show up well on television means more bets. This time I am glad. Headmaster Peeples calls time, and Sylvia begins snipping a 5 or 6 inch branch off the potted hydrangea.

Suddenly, a large commensal of rodents comes scampering out of the kitchen area. The room erupts into total chaos. The sewer smell of the filthy rodents is sickening. Following the rodents are some kind of monkeys or baboons. They seem to be chasing the rodents. Their ravenous eyes shine. They jump up on the tables where the students are propagating their plants, knocking over the pots and scattering the tools. Some of the girls scream. Others faint. I refuse to do either. The teachers, even the men, run toward the exit not toward the students to help or protect them. They leave the students who have fainted where they lay. The robots shuffle in from the kitchen area to remove the rodents. One of the monkeys jumps on the back of Professor Love and sinks his teeth into his neck. Professor Love falls to the floor. Blood squirts down his white shirt. He knocks the monkey off his shoulder, and it scampers across some tables and toward a large rodent. There seems to be about fifty to a hundred rodents. I try to identify what kind of rodents they are as if we will be tested on it later. I see squirrels, beavers, flying squirrels, and rats. Mostly, they are large, sewer rats. Rats with too long front teeth as if they hadn't had enough to gnaw on to wear their teeth down. The rats seemed to be the most defiant, even more defiant that the monkeys. They stay on top of the tables as the robots try to shoo them away. One hisses at the robots like an angry cat.

I hope these ravenous animals don't have rabies. I think.

On closer observation, one is a wet cat. I don't remember ever seeing this kind of animal in a zoo. Some of the rodents look big, black, and wet like sewer rats I had seen on movies and television. It looks like the zoo rodents have made friends with the sewer rats. They probably will be having more babies. I always heard from my grandmother that for every rat you saw, there were a hundred more hiding somewhere. Then all of a sudden a group of something else slithers out of the kitchen. It looks like giant snakes or lizards or dragons and alligators following the rodents. These animals must have been chasing the rodents or monkeys. An alligator might make a meal of a monkey.

One of the slithery reptiles slides onto the table and opens its large mouth. It clamps down on a small wet rodent. Blood spurts over the table. Another alligator grabs the monkey that had bitten Professor Love. This ended our plant propagation session.

Screaming, all the students rush out of the cafeteria, up the stairs and into safety in the sleeping quarters, so the door can be locked behind us. Those girls who have fainted are dragged out by their team members.

Emelia runs into the bathroom, but exits quickly. "There is a large varmint floating and swimming in the commode. That one commode has a rat in it," Emelia screams. "It is swimming for it's life."

I go into the bathroom and flush the rodent down the toilet, but I realize that it may have come up through the water. It didn't necessarily come in the way we did.

The intercom comes on. "Students remain in your sleeping quarters until teachers account for all students. Of course, the plant propagation session is cancelled until further notice and nothing will be televised this evening except the photos we took before the chaos." There is screaming and yelling over the intercom, and the intercom goes off for a second, and then it pops back on. "We are destroying the film from this morning. We don't want anyone to know about our zoo escape. All classes will be suspended for two weeks until you are notified. Boxed foods will be provided and online classes instead of classroom lessons too. We will be getting exterminators from Jackson to remove the rodents and the Department of Wildlife will remove the alligators, but first all of these helpers must be tested for the Silver Sickness. We will get zoo keepers for the rest. Students and teachers may interact with each other, but absolutely no one may come out of the sleeping quarters until these problems are eradicated."

"Online classes? Isn't that why we came here?" One of the girls complains. "But I don't want to be where those rodents and reptiles are, so I guess I can deal with online classes until they get rid of them. This school is kind of like being in jail."

"Emelia, let's go to my room for a while," I say. Emelia looks to be in shock. "We need to let Headmaster Peeples know that you found a rat in the commode." Once we are inside my room, I close the door and open my Pay Pal account. I needed to get a message to my mother that Emelia and I are okay, but that the earthquake has freed some animals from our zoo and that the school is getting someone to catch them. I wonder how the Headmaster and the Governor will announce this to the population above ground. I bet they don't. I wonder about the kids Charlie, Siegfried and the other little boy who are no longer in our regular groups. I hope they are safe from the reptiles, monkeys, alligators, and the rodents. Perhaps they are back home by now. While we aren't required to go to classes, I am going to find out who Charlie is and where they are. I didn't know how I am going to do that without getting caught, but I am going to try. During all this chaos will be an excellent time to try. I think we can slip across to the Headquarters Building where the teachers stay and where Headmaster Peeples's office is and find a list of students names and address and maybe phone numbers. I will get my mother to find out whether or not Charlie is at home or is in the hospital at home. Maybe I can ask that robot about Charlie and Siegfield, too.

"Come on, Emelia," I say. "Do you remember that door beside the elevator? I think it is a hallway into the Main Headquarters and Headmaster Peeples's office. Let's go." Emelia and I sneak toward the elevator and just as we are about to turn the corner, Professor Jay comes through the very door that Emelia and I are planning on entering. He looks extremely angry and stomps off down the hallway. He doesn't even look our way. We slip behind a corner until he is out of view. I run and stick my foot in the doorway before the door closes. Emelia follows me and we enter a long hallway. If another teacher comes into this hallway now, we are caught. As we hurry toward Headmaster Peeples's office behind Professor Elmira James, I rack my brain for an excuse for us being in the hallway. I decide to say that I'm allergic to rodent hair and will need to take allergy medicine here.

Just as we enter the exit into the stairway to Headmaster Peeples's office, the intercom blares. "All students are to exit the building immediately and board the railcars. You are being sent home for Fall Break. Under no circumstances are you to talk about the escaped varmints. This will give the exterminators, zoo keepers, and the Wildlife Department ample time to rid the island of the loose reptiles, alligators, monkeys, and rodents. If you aren't here, they won't have to be quarantined. Stay away from large crowds while you are at home and remember to wear your masks at all times. The robots will give you masks at the Governor's Mansion exit. Also take your laptops with you if you don't have one at home. The robots will take you back to the Governor's Mansion and then back to your individual homes. You will be picked up at the end of Fall Break, and it is mandatory that you return here, or your parents will be in serious trouble."

"Hurry, Emelia. We need that list of all the students before we board the railcar." We stop to listen at Headmaster Peeples's office door. Having said his spiel on the intercom, he is exiting. We scoot behind a curtain that covers one of the large windows and hold our breath. He and Professor Elmira James embrace as if very close friends.

They don't see us, so as they walk down the long hallway, we slip into his office. At first, I open a file cabinet labeled "Students" while Emelia pilfers through the things on the top of his desk. I can't find a file in the drawer with the name Charlie on it, but I don't know his last name.

"Here is a list of students and addresses," Emelia squeals. She grabs it, and we head for the door. Before we exit, I hear someone coming down the hallway. I reach for a light switch. I know this will put us into total darkness. I flip the switch, grab Emelia's hand, and we slide down the hallway on the right side rubbing along the wall until we are at the outside door. The teacher or whoever is in the hallway freezes. I smell perfume.

"I hate the darkness here," a woman's voice says. "I hope you are a person or robot and not an animal. Animals can't turn out the lights, but I hear slithering." We do not answer as we hug the opposite wall. She is as frightened as we are. We exit the end door, hoping she doesn't see us in the light. I fold the list and stuff it into my shirt pocket. Emelia and I rush through the entrance to the sleeping quarters and the Common's Area and down the stairs. As we exit the building, I smell the musty smell of rodents and reptiles. I grab Emelia's hand, and we run the two blocks to the railcar station. We see several alligators chasing rodents and monkeys on the way.

When we reach the station, the railcar doors have already closed, and the robots have already turned off the overhead lights like they do when the railcar is about to take off. I beat on the door. The talkative robot opens it. "You are late," the robot says. "Hurry before the rodents exit The Governor's Underground School into the railcar with us."

"I was in the bathroom," I reply, knowing robots do not go to the bathroom. The robot ushers us to our seats and fastens our harnesses. With the click of the last harness, the railcar goes to total darkness again and immediately it zooms down the track. I hope the earthquake hasn't wrecked the rails. I seems that we may be traveling more slowly. Places along the track seem to have some loosened rocks. Soon, however, we reach the railcar station under the Governor's Mansion. Before we exit, the intercom informs us that we will have online classes to do at home. As we exit the Governor's Mansion, I realize that there has to be another entrance/exit for the Underground School than this. It must be under one of the state's casinos. Nothing else really makes any sense.

"It is a good thing we have laptops at home because we didn't bring anything from the school." I say to Emelia.

Emelia rolls her eyes. "At this moment, I do not care." Her big, blue eyes looked certain. A big smile crosses her face, "I'm glad to get to go home."

CHAPTER 13

Immediately, after traveling back to the railcar station underneath the Governor's Mansion, we are ushered to the elevator. I smell the distinctive disinfectant smell of Governor Wade. Quickly, I look around, but he isn't there. We hurry out of the Governor's Mansion into a waiting white bus. All the others are carrying their laptops. They look at us weirdly, but no one says anything. Once on the bus, the excitement rises. We are actually going home! We are leaving the varmints behind and school behind. I must admit that I will miss the delicious food that was served before the earthquake.

The robot who is driving the white van drives north on State Street and toward Interstate 55. I notice that neither Mike Lawrence nor his father are on the bus. They may have stayed behind to help with varmint eradication. Of course, that would win brownie points for Blue team.

Soon at the exit to my subdivision, I see several cars gathered at my house. Something is happening. It frightens me more than the rodents and alligators did. I feel a large knot developing in my stomach and my heart is racing. The last time I saw this many cars at my house was whenever my father died. I wonder about my mother's health. The robot stops in front of the house near the mailbox, and I run down the steps of the bus. I have nothing in my hands. I run to the front door and burst through it. Everyone looks surprised to see me. "What is going on here?" I demand.

"Oh, Sara Grace," my mother's sister says with tears rolling down her face that catch on the face mask that she is wearing. She looks very surprised to see me. "Your mother. She is in the hospital. She has tested positive for the Silver Sickness." Then she realizes that I am home. "Why are you here? How? How did you get home? Your mother wanted you to be back home so badly. I would tell her, but no one is allowed into the hospital to visit her. We can't go see her because of the Silver Sickness."

"Can we talk to her on the telephone?" I ask. I desperately want to tell my mother that I'm at home.

"No, she is on a ventilator. They keep her sedated because it is very painful," Aunt Marge explains. "She may not make it."

"Why are all of you here?" I ask. "Of course, she will get well," I scream. I want to go see my mother, but I also don't want them in our house without my mother being here.

"We are getting everything ready in case," she replies. I burst out crying and run to my room. I flop down on my bed and cry for a while. Then I realize that no one has followed me into my room. I sneak back into the den and see that they are removing things from our house. "My mother's not dead. Put that back. That stuff belongs to my mother. Get out. All of you get out. Get out of our house this instant." I scream. I have a complete melt down, crying and screaming. My mother would have called it a hissy fit. They pay attention. No one seems to know what to do with me. "This is ours. Get out this instant. Or I'm calling the police."

They drop what they have in their hands and go back out to their cars to leave. I see my mother's fine china, silver, and a box of her jewelry sitting on our dining room table. "Vultures!" I scream. "Do not ever set foot in our house again. You aren't welcome here." I grab Aunt Marge by the arm and demand, "What hospital is my mother in?"

"St. Dominix," she replies. "But you can't see her. They won't let you. No visitors are allowed inside."

"Do you want to bet?" I scream. "Now, you get out too." Aunt Marge is my mother's sister, but they have never been really close. Mom always said Marge was money hungry, a gold digger, but I can't figure how any of my mother's things were worth very much money. Their value is sentimental not mone-tary. They are valuable to my mother and me. Then I notice that my grandmother isn't here and I won-der why. After Marge goes back to her car, I lock the door and prop a straight chair under the door knob. I realize that one of them had a key, probably from my mother's key ring. I think back on their actions. It seems as if they were looking for something specific and used my mother's things as a decoy because our things on the table are sentimetal, not valuable.

I go into the kitchen and open the refrigerator. It is bare. Empty. I look at the key rack. I see my mother's car keys. Her house key is missing, but I know where mine is. I head to my bathroom to take a shower. I'm going to see my mother, and no one is going to stop me.

CHAPTER 14

After showering, I dress quickly and head to our garage. I raise the garage door and get in the car behind the wheel. I do have my driver's license, but I haven't driven in quite a while. There hasn't been a need and I spend time with my friends online. I back out into the street and close the garage door with the remote control. I remember those people in our house when I got home and wonder what they were looking for besides something to steal like china and home decor. Their actions occupy my thoughts until the St. Dominix is within sight on the side of the Interstate.

Carefully, I drive through the entrance and wind my way up the lane to a vacant parking space. Soon, I'm parked in the parking garage at St. Dominix. I exit the car and lock it. I hurry to the elevator that opens to the interior of the hospital. I've been here before, so I know where the information desk is located, but no one is manning the desk, so I take a seat in the lobby. I need a plan. The hallways that are usually filled with people are vacant. There really aren't any visitors. Then I walk back to the desk and take the vase of flowers sitting there. Soon two nurses walk past wearing PPE gear. They stop in the lobby and converse close enough for me to hear. "All the Silver Sickness patients are on the third floor in seclusion. Of course, that is where I'm assigned," one says. "Well, those that aren't in ICU. I can't wait until they get a vaccine."

Recently, my uncle, my father's brother, was a heart patient on the third floor, and for a while he was in the ICU, so I know my way around. First, I will need to get me some of their PPE gear so no one will throw me out and possibly they won't know I'm a stranger and a kid. I follow them as they make their way down the hallway and disappear through a closed doorway.

I hide behind a corner and wait. Finally, the same two nurses exit that doorway wearing civilian clothing. They must be exiting the building and going home for the day.

I walk slowly through the hallway to the door where those nurses entered wearing their PPE gear. I open it slightly. No one is inside that I can see, so I go inside. I rummage through the discarded PPE gear in the garbage and find enough to suit up. Although smelly, this suit fits perfectly. Although at this point, I don't really care. I hope they didn't have the Silver Sickness. With the mask on, no one should be able to determine my age, so I head toward the third floor, still carrying the vase of flowers. Once I get off the service elevator, I make my way down the hallway surrounding the nurses station. Because of the contagiousness of the Silver Sickness, the hallways are vacant, too. Visitors aren't allowed. Trying not to look lost and so no one will notice, I read each name of the patients. Finally, I see my mother's name. She isn't in ICU yet. I disappear behind a curtain inside her makeshift room.

Once I'm beside Mom's bed, I almost cry out. She is lying on her stomach and hooked to so many tubes and monitors. "Mom," I say. Her eyes fly open, but close again. She says nothing, and then I see the tube in her mouth. She looks sedated. "I'm home. You have to get better and come home with me. I can't stay here long because I had to slip inside here. I just had to tell you that I'm home from the Governor's Underground School. I know how badly you didn't want me to go." I squeeze her hand. Again her eyes open. I squeeze her hand again and a tear rolls down Mom's cheek.

Quickly, I grab her chart from the end of the bed and photograph each page. Then I set the vase of flowers I took from downstairs on her window sill. If my mother sees them, she will know that they are from me. Flowers have been our way to communicate love since I was a little girl. I used to bring her flowers that I picked while walking around the neighborhood. I hear a nurse coming, so I slip into the tiny bathroom near the corner of my mother's pod. "Still the same," the nurse says to herself, charting the information with a pen that makes squeaky noises as it rubs on the paper. Then she quickly turns to leave.

As soon as she is safely in the next pod, I exit my mother's room and the ICU area. To get out the door, I have to push a door release button. My timing is excellent. Otherwise, I couldn't have entered the ICU.

As I get back down to the lobby, I slip into a bathroom and into a stall. I remove the PPE equipment, roll it into a ball, and slip it under my tee shirt in case I need to use it again. I hurry out the doors and run toward the parking garage.

I take the car out the exit and drive back toward the Interstate. By now, I am starving, but I am afraid to get any food. It hasn't been determined yet if food might be contaminated. Besides, I don't have any money. When I get to my exit off the Interstate, I remember hearing that some churches were giving away boxes of food, so I pull into the parking lot and see a trailer with cardboard boxes stacked on it. I'm in luck. I get in the line of cars and someone loads a fruit and vegetable box into my car. I drive toward my house through the country along Hwy 455 and toward our subdivision. Once at home, I open the carport and drive inside.

The box of fruits and vegetables is heavy, but I lug it into the kitchen. It contains carrots, potatoes, onions, apples, plums, peaches, and lettuce. I don't know how to cook any of these. I'm starving, so I open the bag of plums and wash one for me to eat. It tastes so sour that I would swear it was picked green, so I put all the fruits into the refrigerator.

I need money. I hear the tinkle of the bell on the ice cream truck. I know I don't even have enough money for ice cream. Then it occurs to me to go to the mailbox. Perhaps someone has sent my mom some money. I need to find out if the life insurance has paid off. I open the front door and hurry to the mailbox. Inside the box is an envelope from the governor's school and one from the life insurance company. I am in luck.

Once I am back in the kitchen, I slide a sharp knife inside the flap of the envelope. It is here. The life insurance check is finally here, but my mom isn't.

CHAPTER 15

I know how to write my mother's name on the back of the check. I've done it before one time on my report card when I made a bad grade at school. I place a copy of her signature on the television screen while it is on with the light behind it and put the life insurance check on top of it. I am careful to line it up with the endorsement line on the back. I trace her signature. Then I head to the car and then to Regions Bank. Before I leave, I get her debit card from her purse. I need to go to an ATM machine.

After depositing the insurance check and getting a hundred dollars from the ATM, I head to the grocery store. I wear my mask so no one really recognizes me. I don't want to be recognized as the girl from The Governor's Underground School. I don't want to be a celebrity. Why I care is beyond me. I head down the frozen food aisle. I can not really cook, but I can heat things in the microwave oven like pot pies, hot pockets, and frozen sandwiches. Fast foods my grandmother would call them.

I think about the letter from the Governor's School that was in our mailbox. I don't know what to do. I hope those kids, Charlie, Siegfield. and the other one, were able to get back home. I'm betting that they are. I need to stay here to keep a check on my mother. Later today, I will sneak back into the hospital to check on her, but first I'm calling the nurse's station at the St. Dominix for information on her sickness. As her next of kin, they should tell me.

After arriving home, I load the frozen foods into the freezer side of our refrigerator and pop some hot pockets into the microwave. While they are cooking, I look at the paper that Emelia took form Headmaster Peeples' desk. I dial Charlie's number. No one answers. Then I dial the number of the nurse's station to inquire about my mother. I need to tell her that the life insurance check has been deposited.

"Hello, St. Dominix Silver Sickness hall nurse's station. Mrs. Carson speaking." She sounds bossy.

"I'm calling to inquire about Mrs. Thomas Freeman. I am her daughter."

"Who did you say?" The nurse's voice is curt.

"Mrs. Thomas Freeman." The woman on the phone sounds strange no longer bossy, but strange as if she might cry.

"Honey, we don't have anyone here by that name. There are no Freemans here. There never were." I recognize a lie when I hear one.

"Yes, you do. She was in room 214. I saw her. I was there this very afternoon."

"Young lady, no one is supposed to enter this hospital as a visitor because of the Silver Sickness, so you couldn't possibly have seen her. Good-bye." She hangs up the phone.

"Oh my. What is happening? Where is my mother? I will call room 214. Maybe she will answer." I dial the main number for the St. Dominix switchboard and punch in 214. The phone rings and rings and rings, but no one answers. I dial the nurse's station again.

"Hello, St Dominix Silver Sickness hall nurse's station. Mrs. Carson speaking."

"Did Mrs. Freeman get moved to ICU?"

"No. We never had a Mrs. Freeman, honey. I suggest you stop calling here."

"But she's my mother. I saw her there in room 214."

"Honey, I'm sorry that you can't find your mother, but no one is allowed to visit Silver Sickness patients. So how could you have seen her here?"

By now, I am screaming. I am totally upset. "What have ya'll done with my mother? Is she dead? First, my father died from the Silver Sickness and now my mom is missing."

"Calm down, honey. I'm not supposed to tell you but some man came and got her out of the hospital. She was still hooked to the ventilator."

"Who? What man? My father is dead. He died from the Silver Sickness."

"I don't know who, and I wasn't supposed to tell you that much, so you didn't hear this from me. Maybe it was another male relative." Mrs. Carson had a little empathy in her voice, but she is whispering.

I knew that if I was going to get any information from her I had to calm down or appear to be. "Mrs. Carson, do you have any idea where they took her? I'm desperate. I'm home alone."

"From something I overheard, I thought it was someone from the Governor's office, but I didn't tell you that. Do you have a relative that works for Governor Wade? They wore white hazmat suits and sounded funny like robots, and I think that she was loaded into an ambulance. She was still attached to the ventilator and a battery when they rolled her out, so I followed and watched which direction they went. I saw the ambulance turn south on State Street at the light. But I did not tell you anything. You hear me. They did not turn on the siren or the lights." She is still whispering so low that I can barely make out what she said.

"Yes, Mame. I think that I know where to look for her. I just hope that she is still alive." It was those stupid robots, but why?

I choked down my hot pocket and opened the letter from the Governor's School. Those same stupid robots are coming to get me tomorrow around two o'clock to carry me back to the Governor's Underground School. That is where they took my mother. I think. But why?

I grab my coat and hurry out the front door. I must get new locks and install them before they come to get me tomorrow. We can't have our relatives or anyone else going through and taking our stuff again.

I must call each hospital in Jackson to see if my mother has been admitted. If it was the hazmat suits from the governor's mansion, my mother is probably underground. "I promise you, Mom, that I will find you whether you are there or not. I will find you wherever you are." Then I remembered that I would probably be in quarantine for two weeks as soon as we were back at the Underground School. That would be a problem. I hurried out the door to mom's car to buy new locks for our front and back doors at Lowe's.

If I change the locks and Mom comes home, she won't be able to get in. I thought.

At Lowe's in Madison, I bought a new door knob with a preset key for the front door, and a chain lock for the back door next to the carport. I could leave the garage door down and lock that door. Then I would exit through the front door when the Governor's School robots showed up. Mom would know the code to the garage door. I just hoped that my relatives didn't.

CHAPTER 16

Mrs. Freeman

The robots unloaded my gurney at the Governor's Mansion. I smell a disinfectant smell stronger than in the hospital. I am rolled onto the elevator near the door and we descended forever. Am I dreaming? Is this Hell? I know I have fever. I need to stay aware. The meds have kicked in again and I'm feeling loopy and very disoriented. My eyelids are getting heavy. What is that smell? It is no longer disinfectant. Robots shouldn't have a smell. It is musty.

The robots roll my stretcher onto the railcar and wait. Why are they waiting? They may want me to die. I won't. I pray.

CHAPTER 17

Sara Freeman

I hurry back from Lowe's with the new locks, and using a Phillips screwdriver, I change out the front door lock. I loosen the screws on the previous plate and take out the old lock mechanism. Then I insert the new one and tighten the screws. I hide one of the new keys in the cabinet where my mother always hid the front door key, but my mother's isn't there now.

When I am finished, I go into the kitchen and take out one of the frozen sandwiches, a ham and cheese one. I slit the cellophane package and place the ham and cheese in the microwave oven. In a few seconds, the microwave alarm dinged. I take out the sandwich, pour myself a tall glass of milk, and sit down to come up with a plan to search for my mother. I need someone to help me search here, but who? Who do I trust here? I thought about the policeman who lives across the street. My mother has a very contagious Silver Sickness. Who could take care of her if she is found? Who would not be afraid of contracting the Silver Sickness?

My answer comes within seconds.

There is a knock on the front door. I stick my cell phone into my inside front pocket of my coat. I peek out the door through the curtain. It is the robots. I need to search for my mother and I figure that they have her, especially since my father had been developing a vaccine for the Silver Sickness that killed him. So I open the door and invite them inside. Perhaps one of them will mention something that may help. I will make friends with one of them.

"Sara Freeman, it is time to go back to the Governor's Underground School. You must come with us."

"Okay. Let me lock the doors, and I will be right back." I make certain to grab my cell phone and another charger. I plan to look for my mother at The Governor's Underground School.

The robots wait while I grab my house key and lock the house that I share with my mother. If she or I don't come back soon, that fruit I put in the refrigerator will be a science project like my grandmother always says. Then I slip the key over my head and inside my blouse. Once we are inside the white bus that is used to transport us to the Governor's Mansion and downstairs to the railcar, I punch the record button on my cell phone.

"Did either of you know Thomas Freeman, my father?" I ask the robots, not expecting a reply.

"I did." The robot that had been taking Mrs. Kendall to the hospital area when I had followed and just before the earthquake. "He was a very intelligent man."

"You favored him because he flirted with you," one of the other robots says.

"Flirted with me? I am a robot if you forgot."

I knew which one I was going to try to get to tell me where my mother was. How could robots be jealous?

We drive back to the Governor's Mansion without picking up Mike Lawrence. I am not unhappy about not having to ride with him, but I do wonder where he and the other students are. Being alone in the bus with the robots made my stomach feel queasy. We enter the Mansion with the strong disinfectant smell by the side door and head straight to the elevator. Before I can think very much, I am on the railcar seat and harnessed with the seatbelt. No other students are on the railcar. I wonder if my mother had been transported by this railcar. I didn't know of another way for her to get to the Underground School. The lights go out and we whiz away down the track. Suddenly, we stop, the door opens, and we are ushered to the quarantine area. I wonder how I am going to search for my mother while locked inside the quarantine area. My heart hurts. I love her so much. I have to find her. Where are the other students? I know that I will find a way.

I am ushered back into the same quarantine room where I had been before with 600 posted, but there is someone lying in the bed where I had slept while quarantined the first time. I think the robots have made a mistake. I sneak over to the bed and observe the patient, and it is not my mother. Tears roll down my face.

I am totally shocked. The patient opens her eyes and looks at me as if dreaming. I jump up and down. She is alive. I can't hold back the tears. Of course, the robots don't understand emotion. They just look at me with their mechanical eyes in wonder.

"Who," she mouths, but no sound comes from her lips.

"Do you know why they brought you here instead of leaving you in the hospital?"

Of course, she doesn't answer. She is sedated, but did open her eyes. She is strapped to the bed with tubes, sensors, and machines hooked to her. I wasn't certain if they were helping her or not, but at least she is still alive, and perhaps my mother is in one of these rooms. I don't know how I am going to search for her with alligators, monkeys, and rodents roaming the grounds and attacking people. But I don't know what to do. How could I help her? It hurts my heart to see anyone like this. I couldn't help but wonder if this lady is still contagious. I'm certain that she is, but I had visited my mother in the hospital not really caring anymore if she was contagious.

"Who brought you here? Why didn't they leave you in the hospital to get well? I know you can't speak with that tube down your throat. We will talk when you are better."

The intercom blared. "Sara Freeman, you will be quarantined with Mrs. Janis Weathersby. Then we may use some vials of your blood to develop a new vaccine. We are intentionally exposing you to the Silver Sickness by orders of Governor Wade. Perhaps you won't have any symptoms. So eat up and enjoy the time you get to spend with Mrs. Weathersby before you become ill and are strapped to a bed too."

I hear a swishing sound and a white and red box comes down the chute. A carton of cold milk follows and lands with a thud. Then a book titled *The History of Religion* lands on the pad with a thud. It is followed by *History of Magic* and a *Book of Digital Photography*. Ironically, I have no camera except my cell phone that used to be my father's. I have not used it much or even looked at the photos on it. They were on The Cloud, so now I look at the photos I took of my mother's chart. All the numbers and statistics are too much for me. I turn my attention to the books that have been delivered.

Great! More boring books with tests that follow. I don't know how I can read and comprehend and be sick with a Silver Sickness at the same time, but at least I was with Mrs. Weathersby whoever she was.

While I am opening the box of food, a robot suddenly enters the quarantine room and administered medicine into the tube that is attached to Mrs. Weathersby's arm. Then the same robot says, "Sara, we must draw some blood from you to compare to hers whenever you contract the Silver Sickness. So please sit down and hold out your arm."

"What is the medicine that you are giving her?" It was the kind of question that you would ask a doctor or nurse that you trusted. I definitely didn't trust these robots or Governor Wade either. I thought about Governor Wade, but nothing really nice came to my mind. All I could think about was that distinctive disinfectant smell he had. It was unpleasant.

"What if I already have the Silver Sickness or what if I have already had it?" I ask as the robot draws my blood into the clear vial. I touch the record button on my phone. My father had shown me how to do this. I am going to have a lot of evidence against Governor Wade, if I get out of here alive.

"It doesn't really matter. We can develop the vaccine using your blood anyway. Weren't you around your father before he became ill? You may already have antibodies. You may be the person who infected your mother. You know a asymptomatic person can transmit the Silver Sickness. We can't know for sure."

"My father had formulated a vaccine before he died." I tell the robot.

"Yes, Governor Wade knows, but where did he put his formula? Do you have any idea? Governor Wade would pay any amount of money to have it. It is worth billions to him. We were unable to find it at your house, and your father didn't leave it in the Pitman lab. Your mother doesn't seem to know where it is. We searched both places thoroughly. That leaves us here, developing a new vaccine. Governor Wade wants it developed as soon as possible, so he instructed us to use your and Mrs. Weathersby's blood to do it. The only way out of this situation is for you tell us where your father hid the vaccine formula that he developed. Apparently, he contracted the Silver Sickness before trying the vaccine on himself. You could save yourself from so much pain if you would tell us where he hid his vaccine or where he hid the formula."

"Wait. You robots searched our home? How dare you? Don't you need a search warrant for that?"

"Don't get all upset? There wasn't anyone to give a search warrant to. We didn't bother anything. Did we? You didn't even notice anything displaced; did you? We found nothing, by the way."

"So who told you to do all this? Governor Wade?"

I look at this robot, but it doesn't answer my question. Although the robots look alike, it wasn't the same one that I had followed with Mrs. Kendall when I was searching for that kid Charlie. Now, more kids had disappeared. This robot isn't the one that I thought I could talk to. It doesn't matter now. I am going to find my mother. I am going to find those kids. The robot leaves, and I began eating my boxed sandwich, fries, and milk and thinking about free roaming rodents, I open The *History of Religion* and start reading. There is nothing else to do. It doesn't look all that interesting. I laugh at myself for thinking one robot was different from the other. None of them have feelings. Or do they? Somehow, maybe? I wanted to hope that she did.

After I finish eating, I sit in the chair beside Mrs. Weathersby's bed and continue to look at the books that had been given to me. I look at *The History of Magic*. I don't really believe in magic, but this book is actually interesting. The table of contents includes a few chapters like the following: putting spells on people and animals, making things disappear, and there is even a chapter about making yourself disappear. It is advanced magic, but this is the chapter where I will start. I really think that making yourself disappear is neat, and it could be very helpful to be invisible while searching for Mom.

I had always been taught by my grandmother that magic was an illusion and close to Satanic. Disappearing into thin air will be quite an illusion. *I would like to make Governor Wade disappear into thin air and not come back.* I think.

The robots keep Mrs. Weathersby sedated, so talking to her is useless. This chair next to her is very uncomfortable, but pulls out to make a cot. Apparently, this is where I am supposed to sleep. I wait for the robots to come get my clothes and shoes and bring me some paper clothes. They don't come back today. I find a blanket inside one of the drawers next to the padded area below the chute. I curl up in the blanket beside Mrs. Weathersby and try to figure out where in our house my father could have hidden the vaccine or at least the formula. I bet the robots were looking for some actual vaccine in a vial. It would have to be refrigerated. I thought about our refrigerator. I didn't remember seeing anything inside there and soon it would contain rotting fruit that my grandmother would call science projects.

Then I thought about where he might have hidden a formula. I remembered my relatives being at our house and seeming to search for something. Could that something have been the vaccine? What were my father's hiding places?

Why did Governor Wade want the vaccine so badly? Greed? Money? The same reason he wants people above ground to make bets on our competitions. Apparently, the formula is worth billions of dollars and several companies are trying to be the first to develop one. I read about vaccines being developed by Pfizer, Moderna, and Johnson and Johnson. I guess if Governor Wade got my dad's formula, he would name it Wade's. I'm certain my father would get no credit. So if I have my way, Governor Wade won't get his grimy, disinfectant smelling hands on it. I'm going to hold on to it as a bargaining chip because it puts me in a better position to find my mother and to get us out of here alive.

I begin reading *The History of Religion*. It isn't as boring as I had imagined. I knew that I needed to read it for a competition. Maroon team is ahead and I want us to stay ahead. I read about Taoism, Buddhism, and Christianity. There would be a test sooner than later. I wonder who would disappear next. For the two weeks, that I am quarantined in the room with Mrs. Weathersby, robots came into our room daily and take vials of our blood, but I never contract the Silver Sickness or at least, I don't feel sick. Their sticks do not make my arm sore. I sit here and read *History of Religion* and watch the patient in the bed in my room. She never opens her eyes. I wonder if she is sedated. Of course, her medicines aren't discussed with me. She doesn't improve, but she doesn't get worse as far as I can tell. I ask the robots, but they don't know why. I also ask about my mother, but they don't answer. Their refusal to answer tells me all I need to know.

Loud sounds come from outside. What sounds like men's voices shouting. Animals growl and howl and more people shout. There are loud popping sounds like gun shots. Then there is silence. Total silence. The robots come in to administer another vial of medicine to their patient Mrs. Weathersby and draw some more of my blood. I overhear a few robots talking about taking my antibodies and injecting them into her. They talk about separating antibodies from blood plasma. They talk about isolating antibodies. They discuss if the antibodies neutralize the Silver Sickness and bind to it and stop the infection. I hear what they say, but I don't understand any of it. Although I didn't feel faint or light-headed, I wonder if I have much blood left. I ask the robots if all the zoo animals and the rodents have been caught. They said that they didn't know. I don't believe them.

****

After I have been quarantined for a week, I hear other voices in the quarantine area next to me. I am thrilled to hear them. "Emelia, is that you? " I ask through the wall. I smell her perfumed shampoo and

I know she's there. Her shampoo smells like flower blossoms in spring

"Yes, Sara. How long have you been here? You weren't on the railcar. I thought you might have gotten sick while at home. I wanted to stay home too if you weren't going to be here."

"I've been quarantined in here for a week. The robots brought me back early for some reason. They are trying to develop a vaccine. Have they caught the zoo animals?" I ask.

"I think so. I didn't see any on the sidewalks or ditches." She replies. Then I hear the robots come into her room, so I don't ask anymore questions through the wall until they leave. I didn't think anyone else was in her room.

"Emelia, my mother is in here somewhere. There is a Mrs. Weathersby in here with me. I just know that my mother is here. Mrs. Weathersby has the Silver Sickness, and is sedated. So far, I haven't caught it. Are you in your room alone?"

"Oh, Sara. Yes, I'm alone. I'm so sorry, but why do you think your mother is here? I wonder why you haven't caught the Silver Sickness if she has it."

"I don't really know. My mother has it. I visited her in the St. Dominix hospital when I was home. We will talk about it later when we don't have to talk through the walls. Did they give you one of *The History of Religion* books? I've got mine and I've been reading. It is not very interesting, but they also gave me *History of Magic* and *Digital Photography*. They are better. Well, as far as textbooks go. I bet we will start more competitions as soon as everyone gets out of quarantine."

"Good, I'm glad you think so." Emelia replies, sounding strange. "You remember that they remove a student from the losing team?"

"Yes, I remember. When I get out of here, I'm going to find out what they do with those students. Did Mike Lawrence come back?"

"Oh, yes. We wouldn't be that lucky. That bully was on the railcar with us. I had to sit next to him since you weren't there. I was mortified. He's one bully that never will learn his lesson. He went on and on about how we wouldn't have won the self-defense competition if he hadn't been set up, and also about scoring brownie points by helping catch alligators.

I survey the white wall of the quarantine cubicle. "I've decided that Governor Wade is another bully. There is no end to the suffering he puts people through. He loves the power and money. My father was a Pitman scientist and had developed a vaccine for the Silver Sickness before he came down with it and died, and Governor Wade wants the formula. That is why he has kidnapped us and has Mrs. Weathersby and me quarantined in this room together. The robots come and draw my blood daily. They are checking for antibodies. I'm surprised that I have any blood left. They searched my house, looking for the vaccine or my dad's formula. When I got back home, my mother's relatives were going through our house, too. The robots said they didn't find it, so I'm wondering if that is what the relatives were searching for. Everyone is so greedy. You never know who you can trust. These robots do exactly whatever Governor Wade asks. Emelia, don't ever trust the robots."

"I don't. Hey, did you hear about Mrs. Kendall, Professor Kendall's wife?" Emelia asks.

"No, what?"

"They found her dead, lying in a pool of blood in her backyard. "

Suddenly, the robots enter the room, slamming the door back against the wall. "We have determined that you, Sara Grace Freeman, have been previously administered a Silver Sickness vaccine. We think that your father gave you a trial dose of his vaccine. That is why you have antibodies. Your antibodies seem to be helping Mrs. Weathersby, so she will be kept here for only one more week. Then, she will be transported back home above ground. Oh, yes. Change into these paper clothes."

I wonder why Mrs. Kendall had been killed and by whom. I wonder where my mother is, but I am afraid to ask.

To settle my nerves, I decide that I will teach myself the disappearing magic trick, so I can sneak out the door whenever the robots show up again and leave it open. I have to find my mother, and I have a feeling that she is in someone's room like Mrs. Weathersby is in mine. I wonder if my father gave her a dose of his vaccine too. I guess he didn't since she contracted the Silver Sickness. They have stolen these Silver Sickness patients from various hospitals to use them to develop or test vaccines or antibodies. Vaguely, I remember my father giving me a vaccine. That is the left shoulder that throbs often. I remember having a nightmare about getting shots. I remember my father waking me and telling me that I was having a nightmare. I remember feeling like I had a low grade fever the next day. Nothing was ever said about it afterward, and I didn't get sick from visiting my mother in the hospital or from being around my father when he had the Silver Sickness. I don't understand why he didn't give it to himself.

I pick up my book, *History of Magic*, and turn in the it to the disappearing act in the index. I find page 412 and begin to read. Someone has taken notes in the margins. I make my own notes on a separate piece of paper which is the way I usually learn anything. Seeing something written in my own handwriting makes it imprint on my brain, and then I can see the notes in my head. First, to perform the magic trick of disappearing, there is a series of statements that have to be said aloud three times "Add 'em. Add 'em, End 'em.", and then you place your feet in a certain pattern with your toes pointing in opposite directions and heels together and chant the same statement again. After chanting the third time, you were supposed to become invisible. I hoped this invisibility worked on the robots, so they couldn't see me. They hadn't been invented at the time this *History of Magic* book was printed in1947. It was written by Bathesheba Bagshot. I wouldn't know until I tried it out on them. I memorized what I was supposed to say. I placed my feet in that certain pattern to practice, but never in the exact sequence that was necessary to carry out the spell.

I wait until closer to the time when I know that the robots are due to come in my room. I remember that they usually come to Emelia's room before mine. I want the door to my room to be unlocked. I make certain that I have my cell phone and the charging brick in my pockets. I long for my real clothes. Searching for my mother in these paper clothes and shoes is going to be a problem even if no one can actually see me. I will feel awkward. My backside is cold from the opening in the back.

I hear the robots in Emelia's room. I repeat the statements aloud as the book suggests. I shove my cell phone and the charging brick into my pocket of the paper gown. I place my feet in the certain pattern. At last, they are headed to my room. They unlock and open the door. I say the final statement that is supposed to complete the spell or magic trick.

Nothing happens. Not only am I still visible to myself. I am visible to the robots. Something is wrong. "You should read your books from the beginning," the robot says. "You aren't supposed to select just the parts you find interesting. Governor Wade wants you to know that thousands of people are placing bets on your abilities in the competitions. You have become somewhat of a celebrity above ground. He calls you "The Poster Child for the Governor's Underground School." He hopes that you will continue to do well in the competitions. In other words, he is counting on you to earn him lots of money. Well, the state lots of money. He also wants you to try hard to think about where your father hid his formula for the vaccine."

"I don't know," I say with an icy edge in my voice. "Are we going to get cameras for the photography contest?"

"No," the robot replies. "You are to use your cell phones. They have excellent cameras. Professor Lamb will teach you more after everyone is back in class, but you seem to be very good at teaching yourself." He gestures toward my notes.

I am ready for the robots to leave. There is a troubleshooting section in *The History of Magic*. I want to know what had gone wrong with my spell. I am thrilled to be getting out of quarantine anyway, so I can search for my mother. That had been half the purpose of learning the disappearing spell anyway. Besides it is fun to overhear people's conversations.

After the robots leave, I flip to the troubleshooting section in *The History of Magic. Rule # 1* - Some areas have been set as magic free zones by a spell placed on them by a strong magician. You may not be able to perform spells there. Well, apparently, the quarantine area is a magic free zone. I can not wait to see if the Commons' and the sleeping quarters are also "magic free." I can't sleep, so I stay up reading the *History of Magic* by the flashlight on my cell phone. Then I remember that photography is probably next and decide to look at all the pictures on the cell phone. Suddenly, I see it. These were the pictures that my father had taken. These are pictures of his formula. I had it with me all the time. This is how I will find my mother and get her back healthy and well. This will insure that the two of us are wealthy in the future.

The next morning, my breakfast drops down the chute. It is a box of milk and a box of cereal. *I hope that doesn't mean that the varmints are back.* I think. I eat the cereal quickly and wait for the robots to come get me to go back to Commons' and my sleeping quarters where some of my real clothes are housed. I'm certain the robots destroyed the clothes I wore here. They come within the hour.

"Do you need help getting to The Commons?" one robot asks. "Will you need a ride in a golf cart? We have brought you a school uniform, so you can leave your paper clothes in the garbage can."

"No, thanks. I can manage," I say. I want to search for my mother here in the quarantined area first while the other students are still in quarantine.

"By the way, Mrs. Weathersby and others patients have been transferred back above ground on the railcar."

I wonder why the robot said this. "I see," I reply without asking. "When will the other students be out of quarantine?"

"In a few days. You already have antibodies. You were released sooner," another robot says.

"Too much information," another robot says.

CHAPTER 18

I spend the day looking for my mother, but she was nowhere to be found. I search all over the hospital and its vacant rooms and cubbies. I look in the students and teacher's quarters. I find a cancer treatment drug, Remdesivir and other information about the Silver Sickness. I find that the Silver Sickness remains two or three days on plastic and stainless steel, a full day on cardboard, and four hours on copper. Finally, I give up my search and go to my sleeping quarters to figure out how to use the vaccine formula as a bargaining piece to trade for mine and my mother's welfare. Using the formula could shorten the search for her.

I consider my options and decide on these:

1.   I will contact Governor Wade through the robots and tell him that I have the Pitman formula or at least know where my father had hidden it. Maybe it would be safer to say that I know where my father Thomas Freeman has hidden it.

2.   I will force Governor Wade to find my mother and place her, well and healthy, back in our home.

3.   I will threaten to sell or give the Pitman formula to someone else like another drug company, even Pitman. Maybe even say that I had been offered ten million dollars for it but not specify the purchaser's name.

Tonight is as good a time as ever to contact Governor Wade, so when the robots come in to draw a vial of my blood. I tell the one that had mentioned searching our house for the formula, "I have figured out where my father hid the vaccine formula that Governor Wade wants, and also that Governor Wade took my mother from the hospital.

Actually, I remember when father injected me with the vaccine, and that's why I have antibodies. That is why my shoulder periodically throbs. My mother and I had been to the park for me to try out for volley ball. I came home wet with sweat and grit on me from falling in the sand and went straight to my bathroom to get a shower. I turned on the hot water on in the shower, steaming up the mirrors. Have Governor Wade get in touch with me. The formula is for sale to the highest bidder, and I've already been offered millions for it, but my mother must be taken home safe and sound. I have to know that she is safe. I love her so much. Tell Governor Wade to send me a bouquet of flowers if he wants to talk to me tomorrow."

I wait all morning. No flowers show up.

CHAPTER 19

I don't know what to do. We will start competitions again in a few days. After competitions are when students disappear off the losing teams. Since the plant propagation competition was such a disaster, I bet magic spells will be our next competition or maybe song writing. It will be something calmer. I get my *History of Magic* book and turn to the page containing the disappearing spell. I want to do this one. I have a few days to perfect this spell, so that I can find my mother without the prying eyes of Governor Wade's robots. I repeat these phrases, "Add'em, add'em, end'em. Add'em,'add'em, end,em." I place my feet just so in the position described in the book. I feel like Dorothy in the Wizard of Oz. I look at my feet thinking I'll see ruby slippers, but I don't see anything. I look again. I can't see my feet or my hands. I'm invisible. I hurry through the door. I do not know how long this invisibility spell lasts, but I'm going to look for my mom while it is working. I hurry past the Commons' Area and out the front door. I rush down the sidewalk toward the quarantine area. If my mother is still at

The Governor's Underground School, she will be in one of the student's rooms in the quarantine area like Ms. Weathersby was in my room. Otherwise, I think they have taken her back above ground.

I hurry past the labs microbiology section, the electric power station and the robotics area. It is easy to sneak into the quarantine area. Once inside, I open the door with a bent hair pin and stick my head into the first room. I think of the Edgar Allen Poe short story about the old man's evil eye. First, I stick my head in Mike Lawrence's room. He is alone in his bed and snoring loudly. Slowly, I pull my head out and relock the door. Then the next room I go into belongs to Lloyd Wallingberg. Slowly, I pick the lock, open his door, and stick my head inside. No one is in his room with him either. I relock his door quickly There is no need to search Emelia's room, so I move on to Jane Ellington's room and Jane is asleep on the cot. There is someone in Jane's room with her, but the lady in Jane's room has flaming red hair, and definitely isn't my mother. Next is Lilith Lione's room. No one is with her. I wonder how they decide who can have a roommate. I'm certain that it has something to do with antibodies. Once I withdraw from Lilith's room, I look down. I can see my feet. The spell is wearing off. I must leave quickly and slip past the robots section without being caught. I hurry as quickly as I can, being careful to stay in the shadows. Finally, I am back outside. I run back down the sidewalk. All the way, I hope the outside door isn't locked.

Somehow it never occurs to me to repeat the spell. I wish I had noticed the time, so I would know how long the invisibility spell lasts. When I get there, the door is open. With the facial recognition, I sneak back inside the sleeping quarters. I'm going to try the spell again and time it to see how long it lasts. Once I'm back inside my room, I notice a bouquet of flowers sitting next to my bed on the end table. That means that they know I was missing. There is a card sticking above the bouquet. I grab the card and read, "My dear Miss Freeman, Governor Wade requests that you meet with him in Headmaster Peeple's office at 9 o'clock in the morning. Bring the "thing" that he wants with you. He regrets that he is unable to locate your mother at this time, but notes that she has the Silver Sickness and is likely to be extremely sick, maybe even dead.

In several days, we will resume The Governor's School Competitions. As of right now, your team in leading. Be sure you keep it that way."

My plan isn't working. I think. *I will not give him anything until I find my mother.*

I feel certain that Governor Wade knows where my mother is. He is threatening me and my Maroon team. I can let anything happen to John Jones or Emelia or the others. I get my cell phone and email the following self-interview to be sent to my email account. I also email the photos that my father took of his vaccine formula. Then I go to my email to find if the photos are clear and readable. I will hold the typed interview in my email account for the Clarion, the newspaper in Jackson.

I record that Governor Wade didn't organize the Underground School to educate children like he tells the public and that we aren't taking regular high school courses, but courses where we can compete. It was set up to entertain the general population and to make him money by having adults in the general population place bets on the competitions between the teams at The Governor's Underground School. I say that nothing bad that happens at the school is ever televised, such as the earthquake that caused a large hole in the kitchen and the escape of animals and alligator's from the zoo through that hole. I tell about the disappearance of children - sick or disturbed ones. I tell about how he has one member of our teams removed to an undisclosed location whenever a team loses. I tell how we aren't allowed to contact our parents once we are in the school. I also tell how his robots removed my mother from the hospital, and now, I can't find her. I tell how my father Thomas Freeman, who worked for Pitman, developed a vaccine for the Silver Sickness and that Governor Wade wants that formula, so he can make billions.

I go to bed, but I don't sleep. I set the alarm on my cell phone for eight o'clock. Ironically, I am thinking about John Jones. I can smell his just show-ered aroma. He is so handsome to me. Finally, I go to sleep and dream of getting married to him. In my dream I'm wearing a long white dress and a veil that my grandmother made with sewn pearls on the tail of it.

At eight o'clock, the alarm on my cell phone sounds, so I touch it off and log into my PayPal account. My mother's message flashes on my phone. It reads, "I tricked the robots into thinking that I was Mrs. Weathersby as we both boarded the rail-car. I removed my hospital bracelet and hers, so they had to take my word for it. I am home now and feel tons better although I had a little trouble getting into the house. Once inside, I found the letter that you got from The Governor's Underground School, so that is how I know that you are back there. Take care of yourself."

I closed the app and dressed in my school uniform, a white shirt and khaki pants. I didn't have time for breakfast since I was meeting Governor Wade in Headmaster Peeple's office at 9 o'clock. I turn my phone off so it won't ring and slip it inside the cup of my bra. I hurry to the hallway that leads to the Headmaster's office where Emelia and I found the list of students at the school. I know exactly where the Headmaster's office is.

When I get back into my room, I'm going to photograph those lists and email them to myself. Cyber space is a great way to hide things.

Whenever I reach the office, Governor Wade is sitting inside with Headmaster Peeples. He is dressed in a gray suit and wears glasses. He has the strong smell of disinfectant. "Why, come in, Miss Freeman. It is so good of you to join us." Then he turns to

Headmaster Peeples and says, "Peeples, could you leave us. I need to talk to Miss Freeman alone about her competitions. She doesn't need to become your favorite, so she won't get any more favoritism. She is making the state tons of money. She has become a celebrity above ground. Everyone has fallen in love with her. We are even attracting gamblers from Las Vegas." Headmaster Peeples looks surprised and rises to leave. Today he wears normal school teacher clothing.

"You are searching for your mother. I want you to know that I have no idea where she is. I hope that she has gotten over the Silver Sickness, but truly I do not know. So, Miss Freeman, I need the formula that your father developed for the Silver Sickness. So what do you think? I will trade your mother for the formula."

"I want to make sure that my mother is unharmed and gets well, and is taken care of."

"Well, Miss Freeman, to ensure your mother's safety, you must continue to win the competitions. People are betting on you and your team. I'm going to continue to remove a person from the losing team after each competition, so to be sure you aren't one of those removed, you need to continue to win. We have at least five more competitions left in this school year: magic, song writing, skateboarding, photography, religion, and maybe trouble shooting robots. You realize that for you to get back above ground, you have to ride the railcar, my railcar. No one rides my railcar that I don't allow to ride. Miss Freeman, you need to win the competitions. Now for your father's vaccine formula, I want that formula. You say that you know where your father hid it. Where is that, Miss Freeman?"

Sara looked directly at Governor Wade. The disinfectant smell that surrounded him was making her sick. She felt like a migraine was coming. She didn't know what to say, so she didn't say anything, but stood looking at Governor Wade with a smirk on her face, as if to say, "Who is in charge now?"

"Well, Miss Freeman, your silence tells me that you don't really have the vaccine formula after all. If you had it, you would trade it for your mother. It tells me that you have lied, so you have a few more days. Then we begin competitions again. So what do you say? Are you ready to win some more competitions to be able to get above ground? Do you want to insure the safety of your friends and your mother and yourself? Do you want to ride the railcar back above ground?"

"I thought you didn't know where my mother is." Tears roll down my face.

"I don't. But I will. Miss Freeman. I will." He looks around the Headmaster's office. "Miss Freeman, you may go now. I will let you know if I find your mother. If I find her, she may know where your father's formula is hidden. So continuing to make us money by having people above ground betting on you is all you have."

"No, Sir, it isn't. Don't underestimate me." With that, I turn and leave the Headmaster's office. *I really don't know how he thinks he has the upper hand.*

CHAPTER 20

As soon as I'm back in my room, I take my cell phone and hold it over the list of students and their phone numbers. As soon as I have it clearly in the frame, I click the photograph. It is the list of students and their phone numbers, addresses, and email addresses and email it to myself. Then I email all the photos of my father's vaccine formula and send them to myself too. I send my mother a message on Pay Pal to make certain that she is okay. I caution her to stay at home. I tell her that Governor Wade may come to the house or send the robots, but no matter what they say not to leave with them. I tell her not to trust our relatives either and that they were trying to remove items from our home while she was in the hospital, so that is why I changed the locks. I do not tell her where I have put father's vaccine formula or of any of the problems that I'm having here at The Governor's Underground School with Governor Wade. I delete all email and photos from my phone.

Then I start practicing the disappearing magic trick. I say the phrases over three times. I place my feet in the special formation and wait. Nothing happens. Then it occurs to me that I need to read the entire *History of Magic* and H*istory of Religion* in case they give us a test and don't ask for an actual magic trick. Finally, I get bored with reading this book and move on to writing a song. First, I write every other line so the words match. *There once was a governor of Mississippi who used your sons To make him money by the tons.* Next, I write the verse. It tells a story of a greedy Governor of the state of Mississippi, Governor Wade, who is abusing children by keeping them prisoner to force them to compete in games. *Governor Wade is greedy, mean, and a sloth.* These games are advertised on television and wagers are made on them. He is making tons of money from bets on these kids. Then I write the chorus. *Get rid of Wade and save the kids. Get rid of Wade and save the kids.* Then it comes to me. I'm going to suggest to Headmaster Peeples that we televise all the competitions. Children will be safer if they are seen on television. Quickly, I crumple the song I have written and flush it down the toilet. I wonder where the septic system or sewer for these bathrooms goes. This copy of this song could get me into tons of trouble. I might never get to ride the railcar to above ground again.

I begin reading my *Digital Photography Book.* I find it very interesting. I read about the difference between digital and analog film. I read about how to use flash. I realize that winning this competition is going to be the most difficult yet.

I go to the Common's Area where I overhear several teachers discussing Mrs. Kendall's death, but I pass on by to slip into the bathroom. They don't really seem to notice me. I don't really go into the bathroom, but slip back toward the Commons' Area to listen to the teacher's discussion of what happened to her. "I think she was murdered," Elmira James says. "Someone saw a white van parked in front of her house the afternoon before she died. I bet it was those robots. It was the same kind of van that they pick up the students in at their homes. I bet the robots murdered her. Personally, I am scared to death."

I slip into one of the stalls and sit down on a commode. I am scared to death too. I worry about my mother at home alone. I need to get back to my sleeping quarters to message my mother again. I say the three words or statements for the disappearing spell, "Add 'em, add 'em, end 'em. Add 'em, add 'em, end 'em. Add 'em, add'em' end 'em." I place my feet in the correct position and wait. This time I look down at my shoes. They are invisible.

CHAPTER 21

I slip through the Commons' Area past the teachers who are no longer talking about Mrs. Kendall, but have moved on to the subject of earthquakes which is just as scary. "Y'all know we are in The New Madrid Seismic Zone or the New Madrid Fault," Professor Jay says. I hurry past them and back up the stairs, being careful not to let my footsteps on the stairs gather attention by being too loud or shuffling. I don't wish for them to figure out that I can use the disappearing spell.

Once I am inside my sleeping quarters, I log in to my PayPal app and send my mother the following message, "Mrs. Kendall, one of the teachers at The Governor's Underground School, was found dead at her house. She was found on her patio in a pool of blood. It appears that a white van like the robots use to pick up the students to come here was seen on the street near her house. Do not open the door to the robots or anyone else who comes to the house. Do not go anywhere alone. One robot already told me that they searched our house while you were in the hospital. That is why I changed our locks. That and the fact that our relatives took your key off your key ring."

I send the message and hurriedly repeat the phrase for the disappearing spell, "Add 'em, Add 'em, End 'em. Add 'em, add 'em, End 'em. Add 'em, Add 'em, End 'em." I place my feet in the special position. I look at my shoes. I don't see them. I grab my cell. It disappears as soon as I touch it. I head out the front door and down the sidewalk toward the zoo. First, I go past the food court and the museum. The gates to the zoo are open, and I hear a kid's voice. It is familiar to me. He can't see me, but I can see him. I see a kid that resembles Siegfield Veene feeding a huge alligator. I really want that kid to be Siegfield Veene, but I can't be certain. The kid is talking to the alligator in an affectionate, but wary voice. I wonder what Governor Wade is holding over this kid's head to blackmail him. If that is Siegfield, I wonder why he doesn't come back to the school with the rest of us, but I suspect that the Governor is blackmailing him as he is me with something really important to Veene. I want to wait around long enough to see who else might be here like maybe that kid Charlie, but I don't stay here very long because I'm afraid for him to see me if my disappearing magic spell wears off. I don't know what frightens me more that person or that huge alligator. That person may be a snitch for the Governor. He may even be a robot. Either way, I begin making my way back to the Commons' Area and my sleeping quarters. I hurry back across the Underground Campus and try the front door of the sleeping quarters. The door is open, and I have begun to reappear. It usually begins with my feet. What am I going to do now? I move into The Commons' Area and wait behind a curtain.

CHAPTER 22

All students are out of quarantine again. They rush into the Commons' Area after redressing in their school uniforms - white polo shirts and khaki pants instead of the disposable paper clothes. There is a poster on the bulletin board of the Common's Area. It is a colorful picture of teens dancing at a greatly decorated room. The decorations say "A Night to Remember." The color scheme is black with silver stars. A prom is planned for week after next in the cafeteria. Girls are to wear formal dress and the boys are to wear tuxes. Paragon, a company that rents formal wear, will be here tomorrow for our fittings and selection. The excited chatter in the room gets so loud that we can't carry on a conversation with the person sitting next to us. In my case, that person is Emelia. The remaining boys on the Blue team loudly complain about having to dress in tuxedos to go to a prom, but the girls are beyond excited at the prospect of getting formal dresses and getting dressed up. The boys are taking their cues from Mike Lawrence because John Jones doesn't seem as upset as they are.

Also, posted on the same bulletin board is a note stating that tomorrow will be a pretest on *History of Magic*. Few students notice this note of the beginning of competitions again and another one about a field trip to the museum tomorrow after the pretest on the *History of Magic*. Tomorrow will be a very busy day.

While we are eating dinner, the television cameras are set up again. We are back to the normal feasts instead of the pre-boxed foods we were given during quarantine and after the sinkhole in the kitchen. After the sinkhole episode and the rodents, I don't think the food here will ever be as good as it was before. I have a very weak stomach. I can imagine a mouse near my food and get sick to my stomach. Tomorrow the pretest on magic will be televised and the winners pictures will too. "We haven't had a pretest before," I say to Emelia. She looks like she has been crying. "What's wrong?"

"Sara, I don't want to go to a prom. I can't dance. I won't have a date. I'm too young to have a date. I can't walk in heels. I don't even like to talk to boys, much less dance with them. I'm going to skip it and stay in the sleeping quarters."

"I don't know what to say, Emelia. Let's go up to our sleeping quarters now and talk about it in private." We head out the door and toward the carpeted stairs. I use my facial recognition and we enter the sleeping quarters. "Tomorrow is the pretest on magic. We really need to study. You never know who Headmaster Peeples is going to call to participate. Maybe it will be like the History of Plagues test and everyone will take it, but it may not be. We haven't ever had a pretest. Blue Team may have more points since they helped round up the alligators, or at least Mike Lawrence did. I over heard one of the teachers talking about it. By the way, I slipped down to the zoo while you were still in quarantine. Siegfield Veene is working at the zoo."

"Really? I'm glad that he is still alive, but I figured that those three had been sent home. I guess he is free labor, like the robots."

My cell phone pinged. Cell phones seemed to be working better down here now. "Sara, will you be my date to the prom?" John Jones texted. I read the text aloud. Suddenly, Emelia burst into loud uncontrollable sobs. "Emelia, you don't have to go to the prom. I'm certain that you could stay here. Remember I've been here alone because I got out of quarantine before you did. Why don't you try to sleep for a while. I'm going to study for the *History of Magic* pretest." I didn't tell her how I used the disappearing spell that I had learned in the *History of Magic*.

Emelia crawls into bed and covers all but her head with the fluffy white comforter. Soon she is sound asleep. I tiptoe to my sleeping area and find the *History of Magic*. It is a thick book and I realize that I haven't really studied the first part. I concentrated on the section about the disappearing spell only. I hadn't mentioned that I could do the disappearing spell to anyone. Keeping it secret but knowing how to do it made me feel empowered. I make up a sample pretest on the *History of Magic* as I read and make notes on the book. This is the way I study. I write that magic was first discovered in 647 B.C. and that the origin of the word *magic* is both in Greek and Latin. I noted that magic refers to a Median tribe in Persia and their religion, Zoroastrianism. This was not something familiar to me. Perhaps I will Google it. When I get to the part in the book about famous magicians, the first was in 2700 B.C. named Dedi in ancient Egypt, but more recently, Bathilda Bagshot wrote *History of Magic* in the Harry Potter series and supposedly it was published in 1947. I find what my grandmother always talked about with the Harry Potter is series that there is a practice of black magic or witchcraft with the use of spells. Grandmother called Harry Potter books pagan. She was a member of the group of Southern Baptist who thought kids shouldn't read about witchcraft.

I fall asleep with Harry Potter books on my mind and dream about when Harry meets Voldermort who is reborn out of a cauldron using blood from Wormtail, Harry Potter, and Cedric Driggory. I dream that I'm there in that cemetery with Harry, but I'm dressed in a gorgeous pale pink, prom dress, and I'm wearing pink heels and a beautiful rhinestone necklace. The shoes prevent me from helping Harry fight, but I do the disappearing spell saying," Add 'em, Add 'em, End 'em, Add 'em, Add 'em, End 'em, Add 'em, Add 'em, End 'em" and placing my feet in the pink heels in a certain position to disappear so I can watch from behind a headstone. Then suddenly in my dream, I'm dancing with John Jones and having a wonderful time. I wake fitfully, see that I'm still in my bed in my room at The Governor's Underground School. This reality is worse than the dream of being in the cemetery with Harry Potter and Voldermort. To me, Governor Wade and his robots are worse than Voldermort and his death eaters. Of course, he is real and Voldermort is fictional. I remove *the History of Magic* from my bed and slip under the comforter. A rose fragrance is bothering me in my room. I notice that there is a fresh bouquet of flowers sitting on the side table where the first bouquet from Governor Wade sat. It is smaller than the first bouquet.I rush across the bed to look at them, but there isn't a card this time. They must be from Governor Wade. Who else could have sent them? The robots have access to everything here.

I slide back into bed and bury deep under the covers. I hear Emelia softly crying in her sleep. I wonder if she is dreaming too. I wonder about the long term effects we students of The Governor's Underground School will have. I close my eyes and roll over onto my side. Suddenly, the bright lights and the intercom come on, "Good morning. Wishing you the best and a very bright future. You should be honored to be here. It is time for breakfast and after breakfast we will have the pretest on magic." Emelia and I get dressed in our school uniforms and head down stairs to the cafeteria. I think about Emelia not wanting to attend the prom, and I devise a plan for her.

CHAPTER 23

The pretest is just as I figured it would be. It is a simple multiple choice test, much the same as my notes. I think I scored very well. Maybe 100%. Emelia and I turn in our pretests and hurry back to the Common's Area to wait for time go to the museum and to select our prom outfits. "Emelia, why don't you go ahead and get your dress and shoes from Paragon, but keep them in the sleeping quarters. I mean, don't mention to anyone that you aren't going to go to the prom. Who knows? None of us might go with the way things happen here. And I will stay in your room with you if you wish, but I think we should get our dress and shoes from Paragon, so we won't cause anyone to be suspicious. They might even advertise the prom and take our pictures for television. Don't you want your parents to see you?"

"Come to the sidewalk out front and load into the white bus to go to the museum," the intercom blares. Luckily, our Maroon Team takes a separate ride from Mike Lawrence's Blue Team. There are so many students that the van has to make two trips although

JO STEWART WRAY

we easily could have walked. I wondered if there are still dangerous animals like alligators wandering around. I know one large alligator is in the zoo and I can't believe they killed the others. Ironically, when we arrive at the museum, there isn't a tour guide at the museum, but each station displays different historical things about Mississippi and has audio information as well as written plaques. The time period of the displays starts with the Indians and some archeological finds of dinosaur bones and Indian relics from the Choctaw and Chickasaw. There is an entire dinosaur skeleton put together in one glass case. In other glass cases, Emelia, John, and I look at beads, pottery, clothing, and arrowheads. John talks about the arrowhead collection his uncle has. Each collection is attributed to a time period that is written on a plague and also, the person who collected it and loaned it to The Governor's Underground School. I wondered if the true owners would ever get it back. After Emelia, John, and I look at the Indian displays, we walk into a large hallway representing the wars that the state had been in with uniforms and weapons from each war displayed behind glass panels. Large panoramic photos of soldiers cover the walls. The boys of the Blue Team and Mike Lawrence climb on the cannons and dress in the displayed uniforms from each war. Threadbare Confederate uniforms, World War I, and World War II uniforms are displayed on hangers for the museum goers to try on. Most are made of wool and look scratchy and very uncomfortable. I am amazed at the small sizes and especially the tiny shoe sizes. Mike and Lloyd Wallingberg are much too large for any of the uniforms.

Next, Emelia, John, and I make our way into a very large room filled with dioramas of cotton fields and examples of antique farm machinery. The quaint farm machinery is old and rusty, but samples of that actually used. Hanging on one wall is a long hollowed out canoe made from some kind of tree. Stupidly, Mike Lawrence and Lloyd Wallingberg take the canoe off the wall and place it in the middle of the floor. I can imagine it being used on the Mississippi or Big Black River. They climb into it and act as if they are rowing it just at the time the robots show up with Headmaster Peeples.

"What are you boys doing? Demerits for the Blue Team of minus 50 points. And Lloyd Wallingberg, you will be removed from the Blue Team. Robots, take Lloyd Wallingberg to the containment area. All the other students must exit The Governor's Underground School Museum immediately. I am very disappointed in you students. Blue Team, your group must load onto the bus immediately, except of course for Mr. Wallingberg. The rest of you will wait in the front of the museum for the bus to come back for you. As soon as all are back to the Commons' Area, students are to go down to the cafeteria as their name is called to be fitted for formal attire for the prom."

"Please leave Lloyd Wallingberg on my team, Headmaster," Mike begs. " I need him to help make the 50 points back. If anyone needs banishing, it is I."

"Can you believe that?" I ask Emelia quietly. "I never thought that I would hear Mike Lawrence, the big bully, beg."

"Oh, I guess so, but not one little error on Blue Team's part," Headmaster Peeples says, "Or you are both gone."

"I can't believe it," I say to John and Emelia. He never would have done that for us. I wonder who he is afraid of Mike's father or the Honorable Governor."

"Why do they call him Honorable?" Emelia asks.

CHAPTER 24

"While you students are waiting your turn to be fitted for your formal attire, you need to plan your prom. You know, like colors, themes, and decorations. Several prom catalogues are stacked on the tables in the Commons' Area. Select the prom theme so that we may order the kit of decorations. You students will do all the decorating yourselves. One of the teachers will be your sponsor. It will probably be Elmira James. She likes to do things like that. Tonight at dinner in the cafeteria, you will place your vote for the theme in a box, or we will let the high scoring team on the *History of Magic* pretest will get to select the theme. Probably, the second option is the one I will select. I like rewarding good performances."

"Well, yay, finally something to look forward to," I whisper to John and Emelia. Then I remember that I haven't given John an answer about going to the prom with him, and Emelia doesn't want to go anyway. They look at each other in knowing ways, so I don't say anything else.

Once we are back to the Common's Area, we begin to look through the prom catalogues. I tend to like "A Night to Remember" as the theme. The colors are blue and silver with a night sky filled with twinkling stars. I think the sky is what I miss most about staying here at The Governor's Underground School. This prom theme has a photo station with an arch of silver balloons against a sky blue background. It would make a perfect photo station or backdrop. I probably chose this theme because sky blue is my favorite color. The rest of Maroon Team chooses other themes as their favorites like "Night in New Orleans," "Mid Summer's Night's Dream," "Wish Upon a Star," and "The Roaring Twenties." This is clearly a lesson in getting along because whichever theme is chosen the rest of us will have to help put up the decorations together.

"Emelia Smith and Sara Freeman, come to the cafeteria to be fitted for your prom dress and shoes," the intercom blares. A sense of excitement seeps through me.

Emelia looks at me and tears fill her eyes. Although I know she doesn't want to go, I nod to her to go ahead and get fitted, so she and I rise from our seats and slowly head to the cafeteria. Once there, we see the governor's secretaries waiting at a table, holding measuring tapes. These are the same ladies who pretended to draw our names out of the hat on television at the beginning with the Honorable Governor Wade Johnson. Today one of the secretaries is dressed in monochromatic greens. She has a big smile plastered on her face and is wearing large designer glasses. One of the colors is lime green and she wears lime green shoes. They remind me of plastic Sprite bottles. Sprite used to be the only soft drink I would drink because I had read that others caused my complexion to break out. The other woman is dressed primly and properly in traditional gray blazer with pin striped pants. She never smiles. Of the two secretaries, I like the one in green better.

They take our measurements and let us select our dresses and shoes from a fold-out sheet much like a storyboard. Like the dress I wore in my dream, I select a pale pink strapless, chiffon one in an above the knee style and pink heels much like the red ruby slippers Dorothy wore in "The Wizard of Oz." The shoes have medium heels. I remember my dream of not being able to help Harry Potter against Voldermort because of my six inch heels. I remember not being able to run in them in the cemetery. I don't want six inch heels. Emelia, who knows that she won't really be wearing it, selects a frilly Little House style floor length dress with lace-up boots. At least, she could wear it if she wished.

The secretaries order the proper undergarments for us for each dress. I get a strapless bra and pantyhose, and Emelia gets a bralette, socks with lace around the top, and a petticoat. Hers is a more logical choice and can be worn to church later if we can get out of here alive to go to church with our families.

I have forgotten to accept John Jones date to the prom, so I wonder what color will accent his black and white tux. My guess it will be black too.

Once we are done, two other student's names are called over the intercom, and Emelia and I are allowed to go back to our rooms to wait for dinner and the scores from the pretest on *The History of Magic*. I so want to teach Emelia the disappearing spell. I know it would cheer her up concerning the prom and being here at this school, so when we get to our sleeping quarters I ask, "Hey, Emelia, are you interested in learning how to do the disappearing spell from the *History of Magic* book?"

"You are kidding? Right?" she asks. Her face lights up like a Christmas tree. "You can do that?"

"Yes, I learned while I was quarantined with Mrs. Weathersby and you hadn't come back yet. I had to practice lots to perfect it. Get your *History of Magic* book and turn to the disappearing spell. When I first tried it in the quarantined area, it wouldn't work because there are certain places here that spells don't work. It is something about being around a lot of iron. It does work here and at the zoo. Hey, I've an idea. Once you learn to do it, that is how you can go to the prom. You don't have to wear that Little House dress. You can wear your uniform since you will not be seen. The spell doesn't last very long. I don't really know how long. We need to time it. You do it and I'll time how long I can't see you. This is to be said aloud three times "Add 'em. Add 'em, End 'em.", and then you place your feet in a certain pattern like the book says with your toes pointing in opposite directions and heels together and chant the same statement again."

"Oh, Sara, I am so glad you are here with me," Emelia says. "I'm glad you are my big sister. I couldn't bare to be here without you." She stepped closer and hugged me.

CHAPTER 25

That afternoon a swimming party is announced on the intercom. Emelia and I hurry to get to our sleeping quarters. We dress quickly in our one-piece suits and hurry across the campus to the pool. The Blue Team is already there, but we don't want to swim with them. I walk to the edge of the pool and dip my toe into the freezing cold water, and then decide to watch Emelia swim. I hate cold water. I had thought the water would be warm, at least as warm as the air. I can't figure out why it isn't.

I will body guard Emelia since the Blue Team has noticed our arrival. I hear their jokes among themselves about how skinny Emelia is. No wonder she doesn't want to go to the prom. Oblivious, Emelia dives into the pool head first and comes up with her teeth chattering, so she climbs out, and we wrap head-to-toe in our large beach towels with just our noses sticking out and run back to the dorm room as fast as we can, partially to warm up and partly to get out of our cold suits and away from the Blue Team's bullying. It is way to cold to swim, but the run works wonders on my temperature.

As soon as we remove our swim suits, we hang them over the rails of the shower stalls. We dress quickly in our khaki pants and white shirts and go back to The Commons' Area. It is empty because the others are swimming or at least at the pool.

"Hey, Emelia, now is a great time to teach you how to do the disappearing trick."

"Great." she replies, looking at me with her big eyes.

"You just say, Add 'em. Add 'em, End 'em,' and then you place your feet in this certain pattern with your toes pointing in opposite directions and heels together much like a duck and chant the same statement again. After chanting the third time, you are supposed to become invisible. "

"Okay, great. How do you place your feet? Show me."

I place my feet in a duck foot position with my heels together and toes pointing out to show her. I instruct her to do the same. She does. "Now, we need to practice. Let's see if we can disappear. Let's go look in the mirror in the bathroom. Also, if you disappear, I'm going to time how long the spell lasts."

We both place our feet in the duck position with our heels together, making a V-shaped footprint and say the chant together. We both disappear. I look at my cell phone. It is 4:30 P. M. We grab each others hands and move together as one to my sleeping area. We sit on my bed and wait. At five o'clock the tips of Emelia's shoes begin to reappear, but she doesn't fully reappear until 5:15. We go back to the bathroom to retrieve our swimsuits to send to the laundry. They are gone. They have disappeared, but I don't think it was a magic spell.

"Well, we don't have to go swimming again since someone stole our suits, " I say and snicker. "Let's go to the cafeteria and see what we scored on the *History of Magic* test." I don't mention the prom again, but I'm very excited to get to dress up and to go with John Jones. He makes my skin tingle.

We head to the cafeteria. It is so cold in the pool that our missing swimming suits aren't a priority. I am actually more than excited about the prom. I am giddy, but talking about it to Emelia would be a mistake. I love getting dressed up. I can't wait to wear that pink dress and shoes. We sit in our usual seats near the front, just beyond the teacher's table so we can hear their conversations. I miss Mrs. Kendall. No one seems to know how she died. The Headmaster clinks his water glass to get our attention. I hear that sound in my sleep. I look at The Blue Team's table. There is a vacant seat like people leave at their table for deceased love ones at holidays like Thanksgiving and Christmas. I think it is their way of protesting the near removal of Lloyd Wallenberg from their team. I wonder where he is. Perhaps, he's sick tonight, but that is dangerous too.

Once the Headmaster has everyone's attention, he says that the winner or highest scorer on the *History of Magic* test is Sara Freeman. Maroon Team gets 25 points. Everyone on the Maroon Team claps. None of the other students do. Headmaster Peeples doesn't

ask me to stand. Then he says that our team will get
to select the theme for the prom. I had rather he had
asked me to stand. I know the theme I want, but I hav-
en't discussed it with the others on my Maroon team.

Then the Headmaster says, "Our next competition will be a debate on the merits of digital vs.
analog photography. The two teams debating will
be Maroon and Blue Teams - more specifically Mike
Lawrence and Sara Freeman. Those two may select
someone from their team to assist in the debate.
Mike gets assigned digital photography and Sara gets
assigned analog.

I look toward Mike, but neither of us says
a word. The Headmaster's rule here is law. I know
nothing about analog photography. I don't want anyone to be removed from our team. I actually don't
want anyone else removed from either team. I think
Governor Wade is setting me against Mike on purpose to get more bets and money. Isn't that the definition of human trafficking? Holding kids against
their will and making money from it.

"The debate will be in two days," Headmaster
Peeples says. I smile. Cell phones are digital. Analog
is the old fashioned way. I know absolutely nothing about analog photography, but the debate is on
which is better. I smile again. There is no way that
I'm letting Mike Lawrence see me sweat.

We settle down to eat and begin talking about
the theme we want for prom. My team is assured that
I will win the debate. "You've won everything so far,"
John Jones says.

"The only way that I'll win is if Mike doesn't follow the debate rules like he didn't follow the self-defense rules. So making him make a mistake is what I will aim for." The team never mentions that if I lose, someone will be removed from our team.

We finish eating and head to the Common's Area. I suggest going to the zoo this morning. I have something exciting to tell the team. Then I look at Emelia. She knows that I want to teach the team to disappear, but I'm having second thoughts about it. What if they get caught? What if they get into trouble? What if Headmaster Peeples removes someone who got into trouble and our team gets demerits like Blue Team did for taking the canoe down at the museum?

I decide to discuss the things that could go wrong with them before I teach them to disappear. "I need to go back to my room before we go," I say. I want to contact my mother. I need to know if she has sent me a message. I could check my Pay Pal account from the Common's Area, but I don't want the others to know what I'm doing or how. I think about how I don't trust them to be able to keep a secret, so I have more second thoughts about teaching them to disappear.

I have a short message from her. She says that she is home, but still very weak. I wish that I was home with her to help her. I message her back to get Grandmother to help her. I say that Grandmother wasn't removing things from our house. She wasn't even there. Before I'm finished the other girls come back to our sleeping quarters. They say that they aren't going to the zoo. "We are still scared of alligators, monkeys, and sewer rats," Emelia says and winks. "We also want to look at the prom decor books and choose a theme." I understand the wink to mean that she wants John and me to be alone together. I think teaching him the disappearing magic spell will be okay. I still haven't accepted his invitation to the prom. " We will tell you which theme that we like when you return. John is waiting outside on the sidewalk in front of the building. The Blue Team came to the Common's Area, so he wanted to leave. He has a surprise for you."

Going to the zoo with John excites me. I've never had a boyfriend like John. I've never had many boyfriends at all. I walk back through the Common's Area. John must already be outside. I walk outside, ignoring the Blue Team, but whenever I get there, he is not there. I sit on a concrete ledge and wait. Suddenly, something touches me on the shoulder. I jump. "Hi," he says. I can't see him.

"John?" I ask. I don't see him anywhere.

"Yep, it is me. I learned how to do the disappearing magic spell."

I am thrilled. "Well, on Emelia and me it only lasts about forty-five minutes, so let's go before someone sees me talking to myself." I laugh aloud. Once we are farther away from the main building, I ask, "Do you know anything about analog photography?"

"Not a thing. Hey, you haven't told me whether you will go to the prom with me or not."

"I know. I'm sorry. But, yes, I will."

"Just in case you are wondering, I'm smiling," he says. "I thought you didn't want to."

I smile too. "Do you think I can win the debate like we did the self-defense competition? Do you think we can make Mike angry and break the rules of debating? You know, they haven't given out any rule sheet yet. I'm certain that they will have rules. I wonder who the moderator will be. Probably, one of our teachers."

As we walk toward the zoo, he touches my hand. "Maybe they hide the removed kids at the zoo."

As soon as John's magic spell begins to wear off, we repeat the spell so that both of us are invisible. We are at the zoo, but there is no sign of Siegfield Veene or anyone else, so we decide to do some exploring. We ease past some of the animal cages, but they know we are there. The monkeys look toward us as we sneak past them. They throw things our way. Perhaps they can smell us. I can definitely smell them. Right past their cage is a door that's propped open. It must lock whenever it closes. I definitely don't want to get locked in here, but I can't resist sticking my head into the hallway. The doorway leads to a long hall-way and at the end I see a set of stairs. They must go downward because there is nothing above our heads. Inside the hallway I smell a strong disinfectant smell. It is much like the smell that surrounds Governor Wade. My sense of smell seems to be keen today.

"Do you smell that?" John asks. "That disinfectant is so strong that it would make you wonky."

"You are already wonky. " I try to jab him in the ribs, but I'm not sure where his ribs are. "Let's get out of here. I would like to explore down here, but I'm afraid the door locks whenever it closes. I definitely don't want to get locked inside here."

They walk on further to another animal cage. "What if the missing kids are kept in cages here or down below. Maybe that is what is down the stairs in the hallway. From the disinfectant smell, I'd guess that Governor Wade is down there."

"Those kids have to be somewhere, but kept in cages? Buried? With the robots? Back above ground with their parents? You have an imaginative brain."

"Yes. Well maybe. I don't trust Governor Wade. It is weird talking to someone you can't see, but not quite like talking to someone on the phone."

"Me, neither. Let's head back before our magic spell wears off. I'm famished."

We walk back toward our sleeping quarters and John reaches down and holds my hand. I don't tell him that my mother may have been kidnapped or even that I think that's what Governor Wade is planning.

CHAPTER 26

When we get back to the Common's Area, I rush to my sleeping area to see if my mother has sent me a message, but I log into Pay Pal and there isn't one. I don't think that she even read the last one I sent because she would have answered. I know my mother. She always has time for me and for answering my questions. I think about sending my grandmother a message, but she doesn't do Pay Pal. I try to phone Emelia's mother, but there is no phone service. I still have zero bars on my cell. Then I realize that Headmaster Peeples must have a phone in his office. I need to get in there. I need to get someone to go check on my mother at our house. I decide that I will call my grandmother from his office tonight. Somehow I must fix Headmaster Peeples' door so that it doesn't lock so that I can get back inside. I look through my school supplies and find some clear tape and some yellow Play Doh. I wonder if there is an alarm on his office door.

I make myself invisible and head to the headmaster's office. Lucky for me, his door is open. I carefully turn the knob and hold it in place long enough to jam the yellow Play Doh into the key hole and tape the closing pen smoothly flat against the door, so whenever he closes the door, it won't lock. I'm hoping that it fits tightly enough to stay closed whenever he shuts it. He will think he has closed and locked it, but I can get back inside to call my grandmother.

Once I'm visible again and back at my laptop, I begin researching debating rules and analog photography to use the time until I go back into his office. I find that Kodak is bringing back film and that 60% of film use started in the last five years. People like experimenting with film. I really didn't feel confident about this debate. I'm tired of these competitions. I need to get out of here and find my mother. Then it occurs to me that she probably is somewhere here or inside the Governor's Mansion.

I research until I find something that can help me win against Mike Lawrence. The rules that I find that might help me are to sit opposite the other team, to speak for the time allowed, to only repeat points to hammer them home, to not raise your voice, to not read from your notes, and to actually take notes. Perhaps I can entice Mike to break some of these rules. I'm so worried about Mother that I really can't concentrate now. I don't really know what to do about her finding her.

I smell roses. I look around my room. There they are. A bouquet of roses is sitting on my counter. I don't know how I missed them whenever I first came inside. It is a message from Governor Wade. I look at the card. "We have your mother. We want the vaccine formula. See you soon." He really is a stupid man. I photograph the card. I email it to myself and delete the draft. I leave the card sticking out of the bouquet. Suddenly, I realize that he doesn't plan for me to ever leave The Governor's Underground School alive. Tears fill my eyes. I must get my mother back to safety.

I still need to call my grandmother. She will go see if my mother is at home. I will do it tonight when I slip into the headmaster's office. I doubt that my grandmother will find her at home. He is probably already holding her against her will. That's the definition of kidnapping.

The intercom blares. I am summoned to the Headmaster's office to speak with Governor Wade Johnson. I remember the yellow Play Doh I stuck in the door and wonder if it has been found. It was such a bright yellow. I figure Governor Wade is planning to blackmail me to get my mother back. I am as nervous as I can be. My stomach feels like it is full of jelly.

I summon my strength from deep inside. I am strong. It is up to me to find my mother to save her. I lost my father. I can not lose my mother too. The Silver Sickness has taken my father and made my mother sick. That and my stupidity is why I'm here. I feel the butterflies in my stomach settling down. I stand tall and straight. I walk directly toward Headmaster Peeple's office.

I walk straight down the long hallway leading to the office and see that the door is propped open leading me to think that the Play Doh hasn't been noticed. Although it isn't the Play Doh that is the problem, my heart is pounding. I smell the disinfectant smell outside in the hallway. As I enter, I see Governor Wade sitting behind the Headmaster's desk. No one else is in the room. He is waiting for me. I am ready. Reaching into my pocket, I turn my cell phone on record.

"Take a seat, Miss Freeman. I hope you liked the flowers. I'd like to say that I picked them myself, but I would be lying. I'll make this short and sweet. I have your mother."

His message hit me in the gut. I had to save her. I had to save the rest of us. "Well, if you want the Silver Sickness vaccine formula, she better be delivered back home safely." I look at him directly in the eyes. His are a pale grayish green today. I would like to scratch them out of his face. I could stick my thumbs in the sockets and pop them out. They are rimmed in red like he has allergies or has been crying. He looks like the nickname the people of Mississippi have given him, but I'm afraid to call him by it to his face. So, I call him Governor Wade.

"I'm in charge here, Miss Freeman, not you. If you know what is good for you, you will do the advertising today for the photography competition, the debate, and win. If you lose, your teammate John Jones will be removed from your team." The disinfectant smell coming from Governor Wade always makes me sick. Today is no exception. My stomach is rolling, but it had started rolling at the thought of talking to him.

"I thought you wanted the formula for the Silver Sickness vaccine." I state flatly. I refuse to look at the Governor and his ruddy complexion and weak eyes again. I won't give him the satisfaction. I wouldn't have made a good poker player. I don't want him to see that I'm excited to get the opportunity to be on television. That fits into my plan and I don't even have to talk Headmaster Peeples into doing it as I'd planned.

"Well, young lady, I haven't been convinced yet that you even have the formula. Your mother doesn't know anything about it other than your father worked for Pittman, but the money you are making me from bets on The Governor's Underground School competitions is making me a rich man. It must continue, and so must you."

"Wouldn't you want the formula to sell? You would be even richer." I look at his tie, not his face. It is purple and yellow striped. Yellow like the color of the yellow Play Doh.

"Where is it? Your mother has never seen it. Or so she says. I will release her if you can come up with it. She is in a safe place for now, and she will remain so if you continue to win the competitions and do exactly as I ask. I've spoken with Headmaster Peeples. He and I think it is a good idea to advertise the debate live on television and we are adding radio.

"Really," Sara says. This is working out just as she wanted it to. "When will the advertisement take place?" Sara acts as if the television and radio advertisement is more important than releasing her mother. But Sara knows what she is going to do.

"They will take place as soon as you leave here and go to the cafeteria. The camera crew is setting up there now," he says. "Sorry. I won't be able to watch the taping. You will make an excellent actress, but I have an important meeting with the Pittman Pharmaceutical Group. They want to buy your father's vaccine formula from me. Sorry. If you don't produce it soon, well, you know the rest."

"Well, if you let my mother go, you will have it," I say. I need to get out of this room. His disinfectant smell is sickening. He is sickening. I could claw his weak, pale gray eyes out. Apparently, he wasn't too busy to come to the Governor's Underground School today because a few million dollars is a good reason to show up.

CHAPTER 27

I have to think fast. How am I going to tell the world that Governor Wade Johnson has kidnapped my mom and is also responsible for Mrs. Kendall's death? I don't want any harm to come to my mother, my relatives, or any of the kids here. I think that I will talk about my father developing the vaccine formula first. I think I will thank Mrs. Kendall for looking for the missing kid, Charlie. I think I will talk about how a Governor's robot may have been to blame for her death because the white van was seen parked outside her house the day she died. Although I shouldn't have to, I think I will encourage parents to check on their children who are here.

When I get to the cafeteria, the television cameras are already set up. They are waiting for me. This advertisement will be live, but it will only last for a few minutes. I must quickly select what I'm going to say.

As I reach the television crew, I am handed a script for the advertisement. Then it hits me. I will use sign language. Governor Wade and his crew do not know sign language, and I'm betting none of

The Governor's Underground School teachers or the headmaster do either. Well, not the ones who are in here. I will alternate the script with sign language, but the sign language will tell my story, my cry for help.

I'm the only student in the advertisement. I'm glad. It will be simpler that way. I don't think I could do what I'm about to do without a script. So I begin. I am so desperate to get help for my mother that stage fright doesn't enter into the equation.

"Hello, fellow Mississippians."

I sign, Hello.

"Please place your bets for the student of your choice for The Governor's Underground School debate that happens tomorrow morning at ten o'clock."

I sign, Governor Wade Johnson had our teacher Mrs. Kendall killed and has kidnapped my mother, Mrs. Thomas Freeman. Help me get her back. I have proof that she has been kidnapped.

I read from the script, "Governor Wade Johnson has given us this opportunity to be educated the way we were before the Silver Sickness."

I sign, "He wants my father Thomas Freeman's formula for the Silver Sickness vaccine as a ransom for my mother."

I read, "Place your bets for the winner. Win yourself some money."

I sign, "Please help me find where he has my mother and free her."

Finally, the taping of the live advertisement is over. Stupidly, Headmaster Peeples is happy that I signed what he thought I said. If he had paid closer attention, he would have seen that what was signed was much longer than what was said. I'm terrified. I want to find my mother. I want my mother back home. I have told the world that Governor Wade Johnson is a murderer and a kidnapper, not to mention if they read between the lines, a child abuser. I have to wait for the axe to fall.

I leave the cafeteria and go back to my sleeping area. It looks as if someone has been there rummaging through my things. They were looking for the formula, but it isn't here. It is safely in cyber space. I am glad that my cell phone was hidden in my pocket because all my recordings of Governor Wade are on it. I change into my pajamas and crawl into bed. I notice that the bouquet of roses and the card are gone.

I try to sleep, but I'm afraid.

I'm afraid of the robots.

I'm afraid of Governor Wade Johnson.

I'm afraid of an earthquake.

There is no way to lock the door to my sleeping area. I get up and shove the dresser in front of the doorway to block it.

I just hope the facial recognition works, but I know that someone or the robots have been here inside my room. The robots are free to go anywhere they wish. There is no disinfectant smell like the one Governor Wade wears.

They could come back tonight while I'm asleep.

I need to sleep. The debate is tomorrow after breakfast. I am not ready. I decide that I won't participate. I am tired of helping the Dishonorable Governor Wade Johnson get rich at the expense and safety of the students.

It is finally seven o'clock in the morning. I have slept little. I bathe, dress in my uniform, and wait for Emelia to wake and dress.

I must tell her what my plans are.

I must not leave her here alone.

"Good morning, Emelia. Are you ready to go to the cafeteria?" I ask.

"I have to tell you something. It is something that no one else can hear."

Her blue eyes get bigger than they naturally are. She is so innocent and young. "Tell me. What have you done? We are in danger. Aren't we?"

"Since we came here, we always have been," I say. "I had to do an advertisement yesterday for this morning's debate. I also added sign language, but what I signed wasn't what I read from the script. I signed that Governor Wade was responsible for Mrs. Kendall's death and that he has kidnapped my mother for my father's Silver Sickness vaccine formula as my ransom. We need to get out of here, but I don't know how. I probably am going to have to disappear. You can help me."

"Oh, Sara, what have you done? That is suicide. You know you, of all people, will be missed. How can I help you? What can I do? Don't leave me here alone. I wouldn't survive here without you. I am scared to death to be here alone." The look in her large, blue eyes was sheer terror.

"I'm going to do the disappearing magic spell for a while, so they can't find me. They can't find me like that. You can do it with me."

"But it doesn't last but about forty-five minutes.

"I know. I'm going to try to make it last longer by doubling it. Then I can hide out. I was thinking of hiding on the railcar, so no animals could get me. That way, if it leaves, I will be on it to get back above ground. It must have other stops than the Governor's Mansion. I must save my mother." Tears roll down my cheeks.

"Oh, Sara, I have to help you save your mother. What do I need to do?" Emelia's eyes were shiny with tears. A large one rolled down her face and dripped off her chin onto her uniform shirt.

"Just help me. First, I'm going to eat breakfast with you. I think that I have time to do that before a railcar arrives to whisk me away. Plus, I'm starving. Then I'm going to disappear. I will need you to let me in and out of the sleeping area and maybe sneak food out of the cafeteria. I may even need to sleep in your room with you. They won't be looking for me there."

"Yes, and there are some comfy couches in the Common's Area. You could catch a nap on one of them."

"You are a genius. I hadn't thought about them. Okay. Immediately after I finish eating breakfast, I'm going to the bathroom and disappear. I'm going to come back to the cafeteria, but no one will be able to see me. Of course, it will cause a commotion since they won't be able to find me for the debate, but I haven't studied analog photography enough to win the debate anyway. I'm certain Maroon Team will lose points and someone will be probably be removed. He told me that John Jones would be removed if I didn't win the debate. If you think it will be you, you will need to disappear as well."

I load my breakfast plate with biscuits, bacon, and scrambled eggs. I drink a tall glass of milk. It may be a while before I'm able to come in here to eat. Then I slide my chair back from the table and walk slowly toward the bathroom.

Something is going on at the teacher's table. They are whispering and all of them are looking in my direction. They know. Someone who knows sign language must have seen the advertisement on the television, but none of them are coming my way to capture me as if I had done something wrong. They can't all be on the Governor's side especially with a murder of a teacher and kidnapping charge.

As I cross the space to the bathroom, the Headmaster clinks his water glass with his fork. "Students and teachers, may I have your attention? We have a problem. This morning's photography competition debate is cancelled." Just as the sentence was said, I felt a slight earth tremor. I look around. Others have felt it as well.

I make my way into the bathroom. I feel that all eyes are focused on me. I will not visibly exit this bathroom. They will never know where I'm hiding. Only Emelia and perhaps John Jones will know.

I get inside and say, "Add'em, add'em, end'em; Add'em, add'em,end'em; Add'em,add 'em, end'em." I look down and I'm already invisible. I wonder if the debate is cancelled because of my advertisement and the signing messages I sent. I slip out of the bathroom and back into the cafeteria. I position myself near the teacher's table to hear their conversation.

"Why is the debate cancelled?" Mrs. Elmira James asks Headmaster Peeples. I think he tells her more than he confides in the other teachers. I think she is his girlfriend.

"Apparently, Mike Lawrence is sick.

"Sick? I see," she says. "Is he in his sleeping area?"

"Yes, he is in bed," Headmaster Peeples replies.

"You have got to be kidding me," I say under my breath. I'm sorry he is sick if he is, but how can I get so lucky. What I didn't understand was why they had all been looking at me. Did they know about my sign language message? If they did, why hadn't they reacted. Why? Were they afraid that they would be killed like Mrs. Kendall? Had they already wondered about her death? Maybe I needed some of the teachers on my side. I know kidnapping and murder would not be acceptable to them especially since they were teachers by profession. Professional teachers want to help people. They definitely do not become teachers to get rich. Maybe Mr. Kendall, who had admitted to making money on these bets, but it was his wife who had been killed. I sneak over beside Emelia and touch her on the arm and say, "I'm going to the Headmaster's office now to use the telephone. Keep him occupied if he starts to leave."

"How?" she looks petrified. "Ask about the song writing contest. Anything," I reply.

"Ok. I will try."

I hurry from the cafeteria up to the Common's Area and the doorway to the hall that leads to Headmaster Peeple's office. The door is closed, but isn't locked. I enter and make my way toward the phone when a robot's lights blink and catch my attention. I slip back toward the doorway and back through the door. It must have been asleep until I entered, but it couldn't see me. I need to get it out of there.

I look down the hallway. There isn't anything to use as a distraction. I see nothing but walls and carpet. Then I open the office door slightly again. It is asleep because its lights are off and aren't blinking. I guess it goes to sleep from inactivity ... like a computer.

I flip the light switch. As soon as the lights go off in the office, the robot wakes and moves over to the switch. It flips it up with its mechanical arm and moves back to it's original position.

I wait. As soon as it goes to sleep, I flip them off again. It repeats the journey to the other side of the room and flips the switch upward.

I flip the lights off again. This time before it goes back to sleep. I know it can't possibly see me. I can't even see my own arm.

Finally, it comes out into the hallway. I go inside the office and close and lock the door from the inside. I run to the telephone and call my grandmother. My father's mother answers on the second ring. "Grandmother, this is Sara. I desperately need you to go check on Mama. I think the Governor has kidnapped her. He wants the formula that daddy was working on. I have proof that he has kidnapped Mother."

"I already thought something was wrong, Honey," my grandmother says. "She won't answer the telephone. I will go to the police today."

"I will send you messages via Pay Pal. Also, I am going to get myself and the rest of these kids out of here soon. He is using us to make money. I know you don't have a Pay Pal account, but we will use mother's. My mother's Pay Pal password is freeman1234. I will send my next messages on it. She used her regular email address. I've got to get out of here. I'm in the Headmaster's office using the land line phone. Our cells won't work down here. Please help me, Grandmother. I love you. Good bye. We've got to get out of here."

"I'll try, honey. Good-bye."

I hear the robot rattling the knob outside the door. I unlock it and swing it wide. The robot clanks back to its position on the other side of the room. As soon as it is in position I exit the office leaving the door wide open. As I make my way down the hallway, I meet Headmaster Peeples who is talking to himself, "Governor Wade is going to be angry because the debate is cancelled, especially since he bought that advertisement yesterday. I think we will go right into the song writing competition and the rock climbing competition, so if Mike Lawrence is really sick... I'm not calling Governor Wade. Let him call me. He comes down here, but he doesn't talk to me. No. He only wants to talk to the kid, Sara Freeman. He won't even let me stay in the room when he does. That could get him in a lot of trouble."

He may not be using his one phone call to call you. He will need to phone his lawyer. I think to myself as we pass in the hallway. My invisibility spell is about to wear off. I head to the Commons' Area where Emelia is sitting with John Jones at a table. I'm glad she has latched on to him. He can protect her from the bullies while I'm trying to find my mother.

CHAPTER 28

"We talked Headmaster Peeples into holding the rock climbing and song writing competitions. Actually, it wasn't that hard to convince him.

"The rock climbing competition is this afternoon. I'm entering it," John Jones says. "Why don't you and Emelia get busy and write a song for the competition?"

"I called my grandmother," I say. "I sneaked into the Headmaster's office to make the call. Thanks for looking after Emelia for me while I've been hiding. She needs a friend. We all need to get out of here as soon as possible. We need to take the teachers with us. We are all in extreme danger from Governor Wade Johnson and from an impending earthquake. Didn't you feel that tremor this morning?"

"I did," Emelia said. "Will your grandmother go check on your mother?"

"Of course. She is my father's mother. I told her everything. She or my grandfather is going to the police. So don't be surprised if the police show up here."

"Oh, my goodness. I'll think that the Governor sent them."

"I hope he gets arrested today. My grandparents will take care of it. Granny Freeman definitely isn't a push-over. Let's get to work on that song. Let's make it about robots or at least something funny. I can't stand any more sadness.

I had told myself that I would not work on any more competitions, but I see that Emelia depends on me and we aren't free of this place yet. Maybe keeping busy will keep my mind occupied so I won't worry so much. I know my mother was still weak from the Silver Sickness.

So we begin to brainstorm topics for our song. Some of them are as follows: Governor Wade Johnson, competitions, survival, dancing, living underground, and first date to the prom. Emelia wants to write a song about dancing. I want to write one about Governor Wade Johnson and how I can't stand him, how he makes me want to vomit, and his underhanded ways of abusing us.

We work on our song for the remainder of the afternoon until it is time for dinner in the cafeteria again. I plan to disappear before dinner time and sneak back into Headmaster Peeple's office again to phone my grandmother again.

"Emelia, would you please sneak me some dinner from the cafeteria?" I ask.

"Of course," she replies. "What do you want?"

"I was thinking about just a sandwich. Or some bread. I don't want anyone to notice, but it needs to be something that you can wrap in a napkin."

"Yeah, I was thinking that too."

"I'm going to wait until the Headmaster goes to the cafeteria and then sneak into his office again to call my grandmother."

"What if the song writing contest is after dinner?"

"You have my song. You can take care of it."

"What if they notice that you are missing?"

"Tell them I have my cycle, am in pain, and wanted to stay in bed. If Mike Lawrence can miss the debate, I can miss dinner."

"Okay," Emelia whispers as several teachers come into the Common's Area. Professor Elmira James is one of them.

Professor James is talking about how Governor Wade Johnson has been arrested. "It is all over the news," she says. "It seems that one of the kids here has a Grandmother who went to the police saying the Governor had Mrs. Kendall killed and some more stuff. I didn't catch it all. Let's look at the news on our computers. I bet she was Sara Freeman's grandmother. Remember how Sara was always getting summoned to Headmaster Peeple's office."

Professor James looked up in time to see me sitting in the Common's Area. I immediately get up and head to my sleep area to check my messages. As I am logging in to my computer, I hear the railcar roaring into the station. It is a welcome sound. We must leave here as soon as possible.

I log into my computer and see that I have a message from my grandfather. "Granny Freeman went to see Governor Wade Johnson yesterday about finding your mother. She never returned. I went to the police last night. He has been arrested today, but I think he is out on bail already. He will probably be looking for you. Be careful, but find out where they are. Granny doesn't even have her meds with her."

Suddenly, the intercom blares, "Sara Freeman, come to Headmaster Peeples' office immediately. I repeat. Sara Freeman, come to Headmaster Peeples's office immediately."

I don't know what to do. I am afraid to be in that office alone with Governor Wade Johnson. I need some insurance. I know that the railcar is in the station. Then I have an idea.

I ask John and Emelia, "Can you get all the students and teachers loaded onto the railcar? Tell them that we are doing an earthquake drill. Don't forget those at the zoo. I must find out where Governor Wade has my mom and now my grandmother, but I know a way to make him tell me. I will try to get an earthquake drill announcement on the intercom. I may have to do it myself. So hurry. We are going to get out of here alive. "

I calm myself as much as possible before I go to the Headmaster's office to confront Governor Wade Johnson. I breath deeply and stand as straight as I possibly can, giving my internal organs a chance to stretch out. I walk slowly toward the office. I can smell him before I enter. He smells of disinfectant and roses mixed together. It is a sickening smell. The smell makes my stomach roll despite my calming exercises.

I enter Headmaster Peeples' office through the open doorway, I turn on my phone recorder and say, "Well. Hello, Governor. I hear you have something you want to discuss with me." I look at the closing mechanism. All the Play Doh and the tape is gone.

"So you've heard. You little bitch. I could kill you with my bare hands. You have ruined me. I will never get elected governor again and for that, your mother and your grandmother are going to die. You won't even be able to find the bodies."

"Let me show you something, Governor Wade. You need money; don't you? Well, look at this." I go to the headmaster's computer and pull up my email and a partial picture of my father's formula for the Silver Sickness vaccine. "If you will let my mother and my grandmother go free, I will send you a copy of the entire formula for you to sell to Pittman Pharmaceutical or some other company. I have it. You have them. You let them go. I will let you print the formula. It is as simple as that."

As I showed him the partial photograph, I could see dollar signs in his gray-green eyes. His face brightened and a wide grin spread across his it as if he could see a way out of his trouble. "Money talks," he said. "B.S. walks."

"Okay. There are two more conditions that I need before I give you this formula: First, my mother and grandmother must be carried to a place of safety. I prefer that they are carried back home. Second, I want to load all the students and teachers here on the railcar for an earthquake drill."

"An earthquake drill?" He looked shocked. "I see no harm in that. Let me get Headmaster Peeples in here to make the announcement on the intercom. You know you can't leave here until I say so. but when do I get my picture of the entire formula? "

"As soon as my mother and grandmother are safely back home, I will give you a copy," I say. "Actually, call whoever is taking my folks to safety now... while I'm listening and then I'll go find Headmaster Peeples to get on the intercom. Then I want you to call my grandfather and tell him exactly where my folks are and when my folks are getting home."

I wait as Governor Wade Johnson makes the calls. I talk to my grandfather after the governor does. "I will wait for your call back here."

"What do we do now?" Governor Wade asks.

"We wait, " I say. "How long do you think it will take to get them back home?"

"Not long. They are only across the street," he replies.

While we are waiting, Headmaster Peeples comes back into his office. "Ah, Governor Wade, you are still here."

"Yes, I've been waiting for you. Miss Freeman wants us to have an earthquake drill. She is correct. We need to have all students and staff load onto the railcar as if we are leaving in a hurry. Miss Freeman and I are waiting on a phone call, so if you could get on the intercom and announce the drill, I would really appreciate it."

"Of course, of course. Excellent idea, Miss Freeman. We have felt a few tremors lately, but I didn't think it was anything to worry about."

The telephone rings. It is my grandfather. My mother and grandmother are back at home. "I'm good," I tell him. "See you soon."

"May I use your computer and printer?" I ask. Headmaster Peeples nods his head. He announces over the intercom about the earthquake drill.

"Sorry, I must conduct a drill and load the rail-car," he tells us and exits.

I find the picture on my email. I send it to the printer. "It is printing," I say, heading out the door as a printing error flashes on the screen grabbing Governor Wade's attention.

He is no longer paying any attention to me or even his surroundings. He is only noticing the computer.

I run as fast as I can toward the railcar.

CHAPTER 29

There is a tremor and the earth shakes. It is slight, but I feel it. I've done some research. I worry that this tremor is real. I worry about volcanic activity and landslides. We are in the New Madrid Seismic Zone. I wonder where the epicenter is. I hope all are loaded onto the railcar so we can get us out before the rails are disrupted.

I race toward the railcar station. Up ahead, I see children and teachers loading onto the railcar. I see Headmaster Peeples with a paper and a clipboard in his hand. I hope he is checking the roll to make sure everyone is on board the railcar. I rush to him. "Are all the students here and accounted for? What about Charlie and Siegfield Veene?"

"Yes, they are here. Now, you and I should load. What about Governor Wade?"

Once we are all on the train, I feel another stronger tremor. Headmaster Peeples reacts. "We must get out of here." I say. "Who is the driver?" I look for a robot. There is one sitting in the engineer's seat, but his lights are off. He is asleep or not functioning.

I feel another tremor.

I smell smoke.

A large, gaping hole has opened in front of the Common's Area building where Governor Wade is trying to get the printer to work to print my father's formula. Steaming lava begins flowing from the hole.

Hot, glowing lava starts flowing down the sidewalk where I ran toward the railcar station. More will erupt from the hole while the railcart travels.

I rush to the robot. Still nothing.

I remember studying troubleshooting a robot.

First, I check to see if he is plugged in or his battery is charged. I plug him in just in case and flip his switch to on.

Nothing happens. Smoke fills the railcar. I smell the smoke from the hot lava. It is a sickening smell.

I flip the switch again.

This time the robots' lights twinkle and shine. My heart expands.

"You must drive this railcar train above ground. There is an earthquake," I say.

He starts the train and just as the lights inside the railcar go out as they do whenever the railcar moves down the track, I see Governor Wade Johnson exit down the steps of the Common's Area holding a piece of paper, but the lava engulfs him.

We travel quickly down the track, but rocks fall on each side of the track. A few small ones hit the top of the railcar. I draw up into a knot waiting for a large one to hit the top or to fall in the track.

We inch along the track at a much slower pace than whenever the railcar came down here, bringing us from the Governor's Mansion.

We miss the track to the Governor's Mansion exit because of the lava.

The robot takes us toward Tunica. I'm not sure that we will be in a better location farther north in the New Madrid Zone. I forget how far the Zone extends, but I think it goes all the way into Missouri.

A kid in the back of the railcar screams that lava is flowing down the track behind us.

We can't go back. Even if we want to.

We travel farther north.

Lava slowly fills the tracks behind us.

Finally, we reach a rail station under the Ameristar Casino in Tunica. We exit the railcar and take the stairs instead of the elevator to the Ameristar Casino.

Lava is filling the train tracks behind us. It begins engulfing the railcars.

The smell of hot lava is suffocating.

We burst from the stairway into the casino. The casino manager seats us in an extra event room away from the slot machines and the gambling tables.

We are too young to go into the casino. Every kid there takes out his phone and messages his parents. They tell them to come to Tunica to come pick them up.

EPILOGUE

The earthquake is so extensive that the Governor's mansion sinks. The tunnel to the Underground School fills with lava. Everyone is glad that we made it to Tunica instead of heading to Jackson. That is an error that saved our lives.

Since no one can find Governor Wade Johnson, I sell my father's vaccine formula to Pittman pharmaceutical for an undisclosed amount. I never mention having seen the governor getting covered by lava. Does that make me a bad person? I'm certain that Headmaster Peeples has told everyone that he was in his office before the lava came.

Governor Wade Johnson is charged with child abuse and the kidnapping of Mrs. Freeman. My grandmother and my mother are safely back home.

Governor Wade Johnson is charged with murder by robot of Mrs. Kendall. His name and picture are removed from the walls of the Mansion and the annals of Mississippi government Lt. Governor Lawson is now in charge.

The Governor's Underground School is closed because it is damaged beyond repair.

G.U.S. is no more.

CPSIA information can be obtained
at www.ICGtesting.com
Printed in the USA
BVHW051433130622
639649BV00001B/91